USA TODAY BESTSELLING AUTHOR
TERRI E. LAINE

Michele @ Michele Catalano Creative - cover design
Sara Eirew - cover picture

THIS IS NOT A STANDALONE -

This CANNOT be READ as a STANDALONE.
You MUST READ Money Man FIRST.

PART TWO

ONE

Time had stopped, or so it seemed. It wasn't just because my car had been the only one around. Or that the rustic and rural landscape held a few community members walking down a dirt path garbed in gear fit for Pilgrims. No, it was like time had skipped over Turner.

My fingers ached to disappear in his dark brown waves that danced in the light breeze. His hair, perhaps a bit longer than I remembered, framed his boyish brown eyes. In turn, he looked me over as if drinking me in.

"Bailey," he said, a nail caught between his teeth and a hammer held at his side. He shoved his free hand into brown britches, which were a touch lighter in color than his hair.

Tall as he had been, he'd grown into his body, no longer the lanky boy I remembered, but a man who could easily carry me across the fields if he liked.

Regret laced his words and I had to glance down, feeling the weight of them.

"Your father's not here," he continued.

I wasn't surprised to see him at our house, despite what my father had caught us doing. I'd been the sinner, the temptress.

Steeling my spine, I lifted my chin and met his lovely golden eyes as remorse grew heavy in my gut.

His pensive expression washed the wonder off my face. Most likely, he was remembering the past the same as I was and all there had been between us. If I'd guessed he would be the first person I'd see, I would have mentally prepared myself.

Words became a piece of paper balled up in my mouth that mentally were tossed down my throat. What could I say? *Hi, I'm sorry I ran off and left you behind. Oh, and our wedding? Sorry I missed it.*

"Can we go somewhere and talk?" I asked.

Wasn't it better to rip the Band-Aid off and have the conversation I should have had years ago?

His hand came out of his pocket and removed the nail from between his teeth. "Sure. Give me a second."

My heart clenched. Its staccato beats stuttered at the thought of what he would say. Although I'd seen him once since I'd left, we hadn't said much then.

He turned back to the front of the house and began to hammer away.

"How long are you planning to stay?" Turner had spoken so casually, it didn't feel like the beginning of an inquisition.

"I'm not sure."

The sun had spun a halo over him like a golden fog. I looked into his eyes and was transported back in time to a memory that eclipsed our relationship.

PAST

Summer was in heat that long ago day, with sweat our only respite. The flies and gnats were particularly bothersome, swarming around in search of their next smorgasbord. I'd just cleaned up from breakfast when Turner came knocking. His presence at my door wasn't unusual.

My being at home this time of day was. It was deemed a holiday, the annual reminder of the day our founders had gotten together and made a plan about what our community would one day become. My body was accustomed to the early morning rise, and this day was no different. We'd eaten and everyone had scattered. I was sure Turner would be sleeping in, not having the same rules in his household I did. As a boy, his chores differed from mine.

"Come on." He smiled, holding out a hand.

My parents had gone for the prayer and state of the community meeting with all the other adults in town. The rest of us were set free, which wasn't very often.

Stepping out onto the porch, I was greeted by a wall of humidity. "Where are we going?"

I was ready for any adventure he had in mind and a bit starry-eyed too. I'd told no one but my older sister Violet about my blooming crush on my best friend. He'd always been just a boy I hung out with every day. But the older we got, the more I realized he was a *boy*. With him standing there, I ignored how weak in the knees I felt by just looking at him. Instead, I put on a nonchalant air.

Shifting his weight a bit, he fidgeted. Turner was always full-on movement. Today, he seemed a bit nervous when he said, "You'll see." He took my hand and tugged me across the way into the awaiting trees.

Once we entered the cover of the forest, the shade from the canopy of leaves took some of the bite out of the steamy day. The encroaching darkness and temperature drop sent a shudder through me. Tales about haunted woods roved in my head. As if he'd sensed my fear, his fingers threaded through mine. Tingles, not having anything to do with being afraid, shot to my belly, sparking a giggle. There was no denying this wasn't an ordinary day.

Once we made it to the familiar watering hole, the spike of fear of the woods disappeared. It was early and no one else had come yet. Most of the kids our age were probably lounging in bed because they could. I, on the other hand, was most assuredly wide awake.

He only had to glance at me, and I knew what he was up to. His grip tugged me to the top of a boulder where an overhead tree branch loomed like an arm holding a rope. With his eyes fixed on mine, he tugged off his shoes and socks, tossing them aside. Then with a wicked glare, his shirt floated to the ground right before his pants. I gasped. It wasn't like I hadn't seen him in his under clothing before but, again, I felt as if an electric charge stirred the air around us. Something was definitely amiss.

His fiery hands joined with mine. Leaning in toward me, he loosed words that both thrilled and scared me.

"My pa is going to ask yours for us to be married." Without waiting for my response, he let go of my hand and took a flying leap, or rather a cannonball, into the lagoon below as I stood stunned by what he'd said.

It wasn't as if nightly before I fell asleep my brain hadn't imagined us together a thousand times under the cover of darkness. Yet, I couldn't move. I should have been getting undressed while his head was under the water as I'd done countless times before. To have him watch me undress was unthinkable. Still, I stood there as he broke the surface.

"What are you waiting for?" he called out with a grin plastered to his face, along with his wet hair.

My heart beat so fast, I thought it might burst through my budding chest.

"Are you coming in or what?" His voice rang out in our private oasis. Trees surrounding the cove cloaked it in shadows with a burst of sunlight in the middle bouncing off the water.

His question felt more like a choice, not only if I was going in, but was I *all in*. I made quick work of my dress, feeling his eyes burn on me. They were like the sun and pricked my skin, creating a need I didn't understand. I was barely a teenager, wondering if I'd ever have breasts more than the tiny mounds that made it only slightly obvious I wasn't a boy.

As he waded, the water rippled around him. I shivered, clad only in my own underclothing, which was more than your average teenage girl wore outside the community. Covered from neck to knees, my arms and my calves were the only parts of me exposed. I dove in after giving silent thanks that my prayers had been answered. I'd prayed that if I had to marry and stay here in this forsaken place, I could do it with Turner at my side. Nervously, I wondered how he felt about it. Was it his family's decision for us to be married? Though he'd told me, he hadn't indicated that he liked the idea.

The water cocooned me in its warm embrace. It kissed the top of my head before totally taking me under. I relished the quiet it brought for the few seconds before I broke the surface. Would I dare ask Turner how he felt, or should I leave it alone?

That question was taken from me when I sprang free from the water's depth and he swam toward me. Again, I shivered for no reason. The water was in no way cool. It had been heated since the first day of summer and only got as low as room temperature at night, or so I'd heard.

"Did you hear me?" he asked, coming to a stop so close the breeze of his words touched my cheek.

"Yes, does it bother you?" I asked, finding my courage. If Turner didn't want this marriage, it was better to know now, so that I might influence my father.

I would accept him as my husband, but not if he didn't want me to.

As was our custom, my hair had been bound. Turner reached around me and freed it. Wet, it sort of flopped around my shoulders. I dog paddled under the water and moved my arms about to keep me afloat. With him so close, I didn't know what else to do.

I was only fourteen, and he was a few years older. When he leaned in, my eyes grew wide. No boy had ever attempted to get this close with the intention I could plainly see written on his face.

This sort of contact was forbidden, yet I didn't stop him. I was thrilled that my first kiss wouldn't be in front of a preacher and the wise eyes of my parents, along with the rest of the community. I was electrified that my first kiss was with my very best friend and the boy I secretly had a crush on, as had so many girls in our tiny one-room school.

Like static, when his lips lightly brushed mine, I got a tiny jolt. He didn't seem to notice and applied a little more pressure when I didn't pull away. Because my limbs had stilled, I started to sink. His arm ghosted around me and held me up.

When our kiss broke apart, I flailed about for a few seconds before I recovered. He laughed, looking totally amused. I pushed a wave of water at him and willed my cheeks to cool the red-hot blooms that colored them.

Turner didn't give up. He pulled my arm, directing me to a wall of earth. It led up to the perch we'd stood on before our descent into the forbidden. Should anyone come, we would be hidden there for precious seconds. Most entered through the path we had taken. Its trail had become worn over time, making it easier than coming through the thicket and risking torn clothing.

The water wasn't as deep where we were, and I could stand. Silent ripples reached my chin, and we continued staring at each other. This was new ground for us. I wanted to ask him if I was his first kiss, as he was mine. Yet, I was afraid he'd think me too young and change his mind. I'd always been that pesky little girl like a sister following on his heels.

Looking at him now, I could see the man he was becoming. Talking like a little girl was out. I lowered my eyes from his challenging stare and saw a hint of stubble on his chin. Still, I held my head high, wanting to stare at his bare chest, but moved my eyes to his. I thought I'd won the battle of glances because he lowered his head. However, he stopped shy of kissing me. Yet, he continued caging me in.

"What are you doing?" I challenged with faint amusement as he continued to stare at me, making me feel more self-conscious.

There was no way my smile and twinkling eyes had said *stop*. Violet had warned me never to give in to a guy too quickly because they wouldn't respect you. Her exact words were *a girl has got to put up some fight*. I'd already given in to the first kiss, but I didn't want him to think my affection came easily.

With a smirk, he confessed, "I'm kissing my future wife."

The way he spoke to me now was so different than it had been even just yesterday. He teased me, yes, made fun of me, yes. But never had his words spiked funny feelings in my body that were weird, yet exciting. My mind worked to process everything that was happening and commit it to memory so I could share it with Violet. I hoped she might explain those feelings later if Turner didn't give me the answers.

While I was distracted, he took advantage and did it again. He kissed me. This time his lips urged against mine. I was unsure of what to do.

Not too long ago, I'd heard some older girls who were only months into marriage talking about kissing. They giggled and swapped stories while doing chores. I couldn't help but eavesdrop. It wasn't as if my mother was going to give me that information.

My lips parted just like I'd heard the girls explain, and his tongue snuck into my mouth and touched mine. I allowed him to pull me closer, liking the way he felt against that tingling spot below my waist. Something grew between us, creating more delicious pressure that made me gasp. His hand moved to my hip and tentatively delved just barely under my wet clothing. His grinding motion was fogging my brain, and I wasn't sure I had enough brain cells left to say stop.

TWO

KALEN

In one hand I held a box; the other was clenched so tightly my knuckles were white from it. I banged on the desk and not for the first time.

My lips still burned with the taste of her, the *lass*. It had been so long since I allowed myself to kiss someone. Since—

"What have you got there?"

I looked up to see the one person in this world I could trust.

He eyed the box in my hand and nodded at it.

Giving in to his innate curiosity, I handed him the model car Bailey had so thoughtfully bought for my son.

"Nice," Griffin said. "Gabe's sure to love it."

He would have loved her too, but I kept that to myself.

I scrubbed a hand over my jaw, remembering the verbal slap Bailey had dished out.

"She got it for him," I admitted.

Griffin's grin widened. "The lass," he said with amusement.

I would regret calling her that in front of him.

He pointed at me. "I knew I liked her. She's a canny one. How did you feck it up?"

I wanted to glare at him, but he wasn't the cause of my rage.

"She knows," I said, steepling my hands.

He waggled a finger at me. "I warned ye. You should have told her after I dropped her off at work, confirming your suspicions."

"It doesn't matter now."

I lifted my palm and Griffin looked at the box one last time before giving it back.

"She paid a pretty penny for it," he commented.

I nodded. She had. In her haste to get away from me, she hadn't removed the adhesive price tag.

Griffin had run a background check on her at my request when I'd considered keeping her around longer than a one-time fuck. There were cunning women in this world, and one couldn't be too careful.

Her credit was clean, her savings modest, and her pay mediocre. But he'd found nothing to indicate she was, as the Americans would call it, a gold-digging social climber.

"If you're not serious about the lass," he said, giving me a wink, "you should leave her be."

I glowered at my friend. "Too late for that."

She'd unknowingly wormed her way under my skin, becoming something I not only wanted, desired, but craved like the air I breathed.

"You're going to be late," he said.

I glanced at my watch. I had to get home. If there was one ritual I kept, it was making time for my son each and every day. I would not be my father, but a better one. Most days that meant dinner and getting him ready for bed. At the very least, I would read him a bedtime story on those nights when work demanded my attention.

That had been the reason I hadn't yet explained to Bailey why I had to cut my nights short with her.

"It's getting nasty out there," he said before switching to a haughty English accent. "Do you require my services for the rest of the evening?"

"Shut up, you arse," I said in jest, getting to my feet. "What plans do yer have for the night? Are yer going to the club?"

Griffin frequented the underground club Connor owned.

He shrugged. "I dinnae know."

He followed me out of my office and down the private elevator. We parted ways at my car and he got into his own. I was grateful I'd driven the SUV when I pulled out into traffic. He'd been right. Snow was falling heavily and already accumulating.

My thoughts traveled to Bailey and how I hoped she was home safe. Or rather that she'd stayed put. Griffin had driven there to make sure she'd made it home and had called me earlier with that report.

I thought about calling to deliver flowers, but held off. It was likely anything I sent her in her current state of mind would end up as trash.

When I walked into my apartment thirty minutes later, Gabe rushed to greet me.

"Da," he said.

He was the sunshine in the midst of the storm. There

was no one I loved more than him. I bent down to scoop him up and walked into my home office to dump my bag.

"What's that?" he asked, pointing to the box I held in my other hand. "Is it mine?"

It should have been her presenting this gift.

"Yes, it's for you."

I set him down and gave him the box he held wide eyes on.

"It's your car," he said.

I nodded. "And this one is yours."

He wrapped his little arms around my leg. I brushed a hand through his hair and angled his head so I could meet his eyes.

"It's not me you should thank," I began. "Remember the friend I told you that would be coming over for dinner?" He nodded. "She couldn't make it but wanted you to have this."

"When will she come?"

Another rule of mine was not to lie to my son if at all possible.

"I'm not sure," I said and glanced out the window, wondering where the lass was at this very moment.

THREE

"Come on," Turner said, shattering my waking dream of the past.

I looked up, reminded I was no longer fourteen. I wasn't that girl anymore.

Still, I waited a beat for Turner to hold out his hand to me as if we were the same conspirators of the past. That day of our first kiss, we'd practiced to the point I'd finally opened up my heart and truly let him in. It had felt as dangerous then as the glint in his eyes felt now.

But he didn't offer his hand. I followed him, forced to accept how much things had changed outside of our route. The years lost fell away with every footfall. *Home.*

Just like then, we were alone. Today, school was in session, and the other members would be busy with their daily work. The place would be ours for now. Privacy we couldn't get elsewhere without rebuke.

Although it would have been quicker to step inside my parents' home, it wasn't proper and could cause shame for my family. So outside in the falling snow was our only choice.

I rubbed my hands together. "It's cold," I said, my teeth chattering as I stated the obvious, looking for something to break the tension.

Turner was already busy gathering fallen tree limbs and putting them in the makeshift fire pit. It didn't take him long to have a small fire started even without a conventional lighter. Flinted rocks were left near the pit for such an occasion.

We sat huddled next to each other on a log. The cold was something I had to get used to. I would be sleeping in a home warmed by a fire or stove. There wasn't a furnace anywhere in the community.

We stared at each other, and flashing warning signs blinked in my head. The name Kalen was displayed like a marquee in Times Square in my mind. I hadn't forgotten about my misguided feelings for him, but I was determined to squash them. The asshole had played me, and I wouldn't let him hurt me anymore.

Looking into Turner's light brown eyes, unresolved emotions I didn't know I had for him surfaced.

I'd blindsided him with my choice to leave. And it took a great deal of strength for me to do so. I'd loved him. He'd been my first in many ways. From being my best friend to my first kiss and the first boy to ever touch me in places reserved only for a husband. He was my first everything.

"I'm sorry," I said simply, twisting the braided metal ring on my right hand.

As if he hadn't heard my apology, he said, "You're still wearing it."

His hand hovered to touch the ring, but at the last second he pulled back. My breath caught because if he'd come any closer, I might have been undone.

He brought up the ring. So I awkwardly blurted, "Are you married?"

His eyes chilled, and since I deserved it, I hastily said, "Never mind. It's not my business."

Though I was sure I'd hear the answer to that question the minute I spoke to my parents.

"Did you think I'd wait for you forever?" he asked.

Gone was the boy who had loved me. In his place was the man who hadn't forgiven my betrayal.

"You're right. I just wanted to apologize," I said quietly.

"For what? Leaving scorch marks on my heart, on my soul from the very fire that had made me fall in love with you in the first place."

My gaze found the ground. "If you knew me out in the world, you wouldn't say anything about me lit fires."

Living inside the invisible walls of the community, I'd felt brazen and strong. Outside of it, I'd felt small and unsure. I'd fallen for two guys who'd stomped all over my heart and put out any fire I had. Yet, I felt stronger for it.

I lifted my head to face him and I met him with a steady gaze.

"You were always a girl on fire. You burned through me like a flame with purpose."

His whispered words melted the snow that fell silently around us.

"Since when have you become a poet?" I said, needing to break the awkwardness that settled between us.

"Since the day you left and I thought if I found the right words, you'd come back."

I wanted to apologize a thousand ways for leaving him, but the only thing I could think of to say was a simple, "I'm sorry," I relayed again, feeling the pain I saw in his eyes. My watery gaze held his for a second. "I was young, naïve, reckless, and stupid. If I knew then what I know now, I would have never left."

"But you did."

Again, the temperature between us cooled and I couldn't blame him.

I looked down at myself, though wrapped in a coat, and pictured how far I'd come from the flat-chested girl he'd fallen for to where I was now full of curves. That girl wouldn't have been wearing the blue lace bra and panties I wore underneath it all. Nor could that girl have ever met the likes of the man who'd bought them.

One thing I'd done in anticipation of my return was pull my hair back into the required bun. Turner reached out and gently brushed his calloused fingertips across my cheek, sending quivers through me before he pulled my hair free.

"I wanted to hate you," he admitted. "You didn't trust me enough to tell me first. You were just gone."

I squeezed my lids shut and answered honestly. "I was a coward."

I'd also been scared. One thing he hadn't taken into account was that we didn't have a lot of alone time as we got older. It wasn't proper. The stolen moments we did have had been spent doing other pleasurable things when conversation hadn't been high on our list.

"You were," he agreed, never one to mince words.

He deserved the truth of all of it. "I was, but I wasn't afraid to tell you I was leaving as much as I was afraid you'd ask me to stay, which I would have."

We held there for a second in suspended silence.

"I would have supported you. I would have even gone with you."

That last part surprised me.

"But you love this place," I protested, more because I hated knowing that I might have made a grave mistake.

"I do. But I loved you more. I'd been taking online college classes and you knew that."

I ignored his use of the past tense. Instead, I focused on the rest.

Our community leaders encouraged a select few to take college courses and get degrees. They were forward thinking enough to know we had businesses to run for our survival. That meant trading with the secular world. We needed educated people to negotiate so that we weren't seen as some backwards community.

"I did. But—" I began.

"You didn't trust me with your dreams. If you had, maybe you would have understood mine, and my reasons for staying were for you."

Ashamed and doubting myself again, I felt tears prickle the corners of my eyes.

He leaned back and faced the fire, stretching out his arms to warm his hands.

"I left shortly after you did and attended Penn State University."

My eyes widened and I wanted to congratulate and hug

him. Something in his gaze stopped me and understood why he'd put distance between us.

Lost, I watched helplessly as he stood and dusted himself off. The air between us felt like ice against my skin, but I made no attempt to move.

I'd said my piece. I'd given him my truth. That weight was lifted off me.

He would either forgive me or he wouldn't. I wouldn't chase him to change his mind. I let him walk away.

One last time, I let the tears spill from my eyes and I mused over the mess my life was. It felt like I'd lost two men I cared about in one day.

But this was the last time I would cry over either of them. Especially the turd. He could take his lass and shove it as I wondered what he was doing at that very moment.

FOUR

KALEN

BAILEY. THE BEGUILING WOMAN HAD CONSUMED MY thoughts since she walked out of my office door.

Snow was still falling in heavy clumps when I pulled out into traffic in my Range Rower prepared for the weather.

Traffic was stalled, but I made decent time to Bailey's apartment. I accessed the garage because I owned several apartments that I rented out in the building. Another thing I needed to explain to the woman who thought me a liar.

I barely got a hand up to knock on the door when it opened.

Lizzy stopped short with a hand to her chest.

"Jesus, you scared me," she said pleasantly.

For a second, I had hope that Bailey's temper had calmed and maybe she was ready to listen to reason.

I got down to business. "Is she here?"

Bailey's best friend immediately went on guard dog duty. Her eyes narrowed and her jaw tightened.

"And if she was, do you think I'd tell you?"

"Look, I need to talk to her," I said, angling to see inside, hoping to catch sight of Bailey on the sofa.

Lizzy shifted to obstruct my view.

"She was very clear she doesn't want to see you, *Jeremy King*."

Her brow arched in a clear challenge.

I sighed and let my eyes drop. That's when I noticed the suitcase at her side. I snapped my head up to meet her gaze.

"Where are you going?"

She lifted her chin. "That's really none of your business. Besides, you out of everyone should understand the fine art of withholding information."

I was a man who hadn't begged for anything in my life even when I was starving in the streets of Edinburg. But I humbled myself before Bailey's gatekeeper.

"I really need to talk to her."

She eyed me a second before speaking. "She's not here."

"Tell me where she is. Are you going to meet her?"

"No," she said, and I believed her. "You need to give her time. If she wants to talk to you, she'll contact you."

She pulled out her phone and I thought she was going to call Bailey. Instead, she lifted it and the sound of snapping a picture broke the silence.

Her face lit up with a grin. "And if you don't give her space, I'll be sure to post this all over the web. The elusive Jeremey King, Money Man, or Lying Thief, whatever they call you. And if you're going to give yourself an alias, drop the n out of Kalen. Kale is more your speed. You know, the thing nobody really wants."

She stepped back and closed the door in my face. I stood there for a second, uncaring about the picture. For so long I'd hidden in the shadows per my father's wishes. Where had that gotten me?

I placed my palm flat against the door, wondering if Lizzy had been lying. Was Bailey behind the door? I almost knocked, unsure what to do in this situation. Never once had I ever wanted a woman enough to fight for her.

A moment later and I straightened. I'd give Lizzy's advice a trial period. I could give Bailey time. I owed her that much, and more.

For now, I'd go home. I had plans to make for the future.

FIVE

By the time I made it to my parents' place, I was frozen. I walked straight into the house, as doors weren't normally kept locked, and headed into my old room. I found a towel and dried my snow-covered hair as best I could. I'd donned a bonnet I found and warmed myself by the large cast iron stove before heading off to the place that gave me the most comfort outside of home.

Every other woman in town that I passed was garbed in similar clothing, except for my coat. Many gave me curious glances but said nothing outside of a polite greeting. I slipped into the schoolhouse office without my younger siblings noticing. I got a nod from the head teacher before I was behind the closed door.

I sat at the big desk and wondered where my older sister Violet was. I was out of sorts and needed someone I could trust to talk to. But she was working, and it would be frowned upon for me to interrupt, so I stayed put.

It was easy to slip into the familiar. I dived in using my auditing skills to continue to review the community's books. It was something unique I could offer, so I did it without being asked. It was doubtful my replacement, which was the woman who apprenticed me, would be doing anything wrong. It was just something to keep me busy.

My focus kept shifting between the phone and the ledgers over and over again. Out of three ruined relationships, I was the only common denominator. Maybe Scott was right. It was me all along.

Hesitantly, I picked up the faded moss green colored handset from the cradle and pushed the buttons on the base. Our phones had non-registered numbers and would display UNKNOWN as the caller. I wasn't sure if my call would be answered.

"Hello."

"Lizzy," I said on an exhale of relief.

"Oh my God, honey. Are you okay?"

There was noise in the background.

"I'm fine. Where are you?"

"At the airport. I'm going to Chicago to see that artist, Haven. I want to commission more of her work. Plus, I want to check up on Matt."

"Oh," I said, feeling sorry for myself.

Lizzy's life was moving forward, while mine was moving backward.

"Did you make it home?" she asked. "I got your message and I'm worried about you driving in that weather."

"It's fine. I'm here."

"They have phones?" she asked, sounding utterly shocked.

I let out a bitter laugh. "Yeah, and a couple of

computers too. Though we aren't allowed to use them regularly. I should probably cut this short."

"Don't go. Your stalker stopped by."

My heart did a little traitorous pitter-patter.

"He didn't," I said, not sure why I was surprised.

The man was used to getting what he wanted. The only reason he was pursuing me was because I was probably the first woman to tell him no.

"He did with damnable puppy dog eyes. You should have seen him. I almost gave in."

"You didn't," I warned even though it would have been too late as I tried and failed to imagine puppy dog eyes on the arrogant bastard.

"I didn't," she agreed. "I gave him hell. But sweetie, I hate to say this because I'm totally on your side. But he had the look of a man in love."

I rolled my eyes. "That look is someone who isn't used to losing."

"If you say so. If I were a betting woman, I'd say he's got it bad for you."

For a second, I felt my resolve wavering, but I pushed past it.

"Good thing you don't bet," I said. "Give my love to Matt."

She laughed. "I will not. That would give him hope. And we both know you've got it *bad* for a certain King," she teased in a sing-song voice.

"Not anymore," I muttered, unable to completely lie.

"You can lie to yourself but not to me. Anywho, they are boarding my plane."

"You're flying commercial?" I asked.

"Damn right. You see this weather. I want someone solid to fly me in these unfriendly skies. Oh, before I go. You got roses."

I blew out a breath. "From him."

"I don't think so. He didn't mention them, and they were black roses. Weird, huh?" A chill ran up my spine. "I imagine they will die a timely death before you can see them. I took a picture for you, though."

"No message?" I asked, my mouth feeling suddenly dry.

"None," she said.

"Safe travels," I added, with a little cheer. I missed her so much already. "I'll try to call you in a few days. I don't have my cell so you can't call me."

"You know how weird that is, right?" she asked.

"I do."

"You stay safe too. Be sure to check in or *I'll have my brother find you*," she teased.

"Bye," I said and she said it back.

When I placed the handset back on the base, I felt alone. Though I'd been close to my sister Violet, she and I were very different people. Lizzy had been a kindred spirit of sorts even though we'd grown up with very different lives.

Then my inconsiderate thoughts drifted back to Kalen, the virile man. He wouldn't be lonely for long. Women would line up to play bedmate. And I'd freed him, not that he was the kind of man to be tethered to anyone. So why should I think of him?

I was glad there wasn't access to TVs or social media. Though I'd given him up, it wasn't like I could handle seeing him with someone else.

Thinking of him only made my nether regions clench in

anticipation. Memories of how he buried himself inside me and how he knew exactly how to wield that big cock of his almost made me whimper until I checked myself. No. I was strong. Screw him, as Lizzy would say. Then again, those words were the exact cause of all my troubles.

Those events had led me here and had solidified our non-future. I tucked all thoughts of Kalen away and wouldn't name what I felt for him. Anger, lov—It didn't matter. It was one too many emotions wasted on a man who didn't deserve my time.

Instead, I dug back into the financial status of the community, relentlessly checking every transaction recorded to a source document like bank deposits and invoices as if I were still an auditor for a powerful international accounting firm.

The passage of time was counted by the dimming light trailing through the tiny window above the desk. I'd lit a candle earlier when the light had begun to fade. Now the room cloaked in shadows felt smaller and more cramped in the disappearing light.

A desk, chair, and one of the two telephones in the compound filled the room. The only other piece of furniture was a bookshelf that anchored one end of the room and held the weight of the community's manual book-keeping.

It seemed my arrival hadn't been shared with my school-bound siblings as they hadn't come to see me. But then again, my arrival was probably not the highlight of their day.

My skin nearly left my body when a voice broke through the silence. "I thought you'd be here."

There was no need to see Turner standing behind me. His voice would always and forever be familiar to me.

"Hey," I said before a yawn escaped my lips. The flickering candlelight gave the room an ethereal glow.

One thing hadn't changed. He didn't hold fast to anger long if his appearance here was any indication.

"Burning the night away?" he asked. "Or are you just hiding from me or maybe your father?"

It was both. However, I kept that to myself. After he left earlier, I wasn't sure if he'd want to talk to me. A smile found its way to dance across my lips when I turned to face his grin.

It was true. He'd said his piece and wasn't holding a grudge. Ignoring part of his question, I said, "I'm hoping maybe Father will be asleep before I make it home."

He held a hand out to me. "You know your father. If he wants to talk to you tonight, he'll wait up. You might as well get it over with."

A groan left me before I took his hand and let him draw me to my feet. "I should go see Violet before it gets too late," I said, closing the ledgers and putting them back on the shelf.

"You should wait until tomorrow. It's late and it would be a long walk to her place," he said.

I faced Turner to see he hadn't moved. The expression on his face was tight. The tension between us was back, and I wasn't sure what to make of it. There was no denying the attraction I felt to him or the love that swelled in my heart. I'd known him all my life. At one time, I wanted to be his wife. But now... now I wasn't sure. Everything was mottled because of Kalen. There was something about that man I couldn't explain.

Warm hands wrapped around my arms, bringing me back. I looked up into those fathomless warm brown eyes almost the color of amber. "Turner."

He took my calling out his name as an invitation, because his mouth headed toward mine.

SIX

KALEN

THE ARROGANCE OF THE ACCOUNTING CLERK WHO SAT before me knew no bounds. You would have thought he was the boss given the smirk on his face.

"Who authorized this wire?" I asked again.

"You," he said with the utmost confidence. "I forwarded you the emails I received from you telling me to make those transfers."

I didn't have to glance at my screen. I'd already seen the evidence, but I'd wanted to size the man up for myself.

"Going forward, no wires or transfers are to be made without verbal authorization from me."

The smirk disappeared. "What about—"

I waved him off. "If any transfers are made without my verbal authority, the person who did it will be fired."

The satisfaction I got out of watching the smugness leave his face caused my mouth to curl into a wicked grin.

"Close the door on the way out," I added.

Once he was gone, I picked up my phone and dialed Griffin.

"Yo," he said.

"Are you an American now?"

He chuckled. "When in America..."

I ignored him. "I need you to have your people look into my email account. On the surface it appears I sent emails to the accounting department directing them to wire money to offshore accounts. Find out where they originated. Then I want you to do a background check on everyone in the accounting department."

After leaving the Special Forces, Griffin built a company from the ground up that specialized in physical and cybersecurity.

"You think this is an inside job?" he asked.

"I think there's someone out to destroy my name."

"Or just good old-fashioned thievery?" he guessed.

I wasn't buying it.

"Someone is going through an awful lot of trouble."

"Do you think it's—"

"No," I said immediately without thought.

"Maybe I should look into it?" His brow quirked. "Bailey could be in danger."

The thought had crossed my mind. Once she'd mentioned a note she thought someone I knew had sent her.

"I dinnae ken," I said, falling into the familiar cadence of home.

"Do you want me to follow her?"

Where there might have been humor, like when I'd asked him to play driver, he sounded serious.

"If I knew where she was."

He swore, "Do you want me to find her?"

It had only been a few days and I hadn't wanted to pull that trigger.

"Dinnae be a bampot," he cursed.

Hearing his concern, I gave him the only answer I could. "Aye. Find the lass."

But what to do when she was found?

SEVEN

Before Turner's lips touched mine, I stepped back and shook my head.

"We shouldn't," I said, unsure, sounding small, but glad it came out firm.

My reasoning was sound. I wouldn't leapfrog into another man's arms. Especially when he would make it too darn easy.

His hands dropped from my waist.

"Sorry," he said, his eyes finding the ground. "I'll walk you home then," he suggested.

"Maybe I should stop by Mary's and see the baby." Even to my own ears, I could hear the excuse, as he probably could.

I might have stopped that first kiss, but I was drawn to Turner like a moth to a flame. And maybe he was the best man for me. I couldn't be sure as long as my feelings were still twisted in my heart. I needed time. Time I hadn't taken to get over Turner and ended up in a disastrous relationship with Scott.

Turner quirked a brow. "Are you afraid of me?"

"I'm not," I said adamantly with my hands folded over my chest.

I would never be afraid of him, but I did feel way too vulnerable and moved out of the confining room into the larger classroom. My hand lovingly ran across the top of the wooden desk I'd sat at so very long ago.

Stepping out into the night, I found the dark all-encompassing. It was so very different than the city that never slept. Tonight, a blanket of clouds hid the stars and the moon. I stood in place, looked up, and breathed in deeply. The air was so very different here, free of smog and other pollutants.

"You miss it," Turner said, breaking into my thoughts.

Slowly, I lowered my head to meet his eyes, but not too much considering Turner was far taller than me. "Maybe," I confessed. "You?"

A tiny smile crept onto his face, reluctant and wary. "I missed you."

A wave of emotion ran through me, making it hard to ignore the gorgeous guy in front of me. Despite my protest a minute ago, I couldn't help what happened next. As inadvisable as it was, I reached out a hand to touch his cheek. He leaned into it. In that moment, all the memories we shared flashed across my mind.

Memories had me unconsciously on my toes, leaning up to place a heartfelt kiss on his cheek. It was a bad idea for many reasons, especially when he turned, allowing our lips to brush across one another's.

Turner felt like home and it would be too easy to lose myself in his touch, his embrace, and his kiss. Thus, I dropped back to my feet and tucked a wayward strand of hair behind my ear, unable to meet his gaze.

When I did, his easy smile was in full bloom. He took my hand in his like a schoolboy with his first crush and gave it a little squeeze.

"Daughter."

We turned as a unit to face my father. In typical fashion, he wore a hat that crowned his head. His beard, which had been the same burnt orange as my hair, speckled with gray.

"Father," I said respectfully, bowing my head and quickly letting go of Turner's hand.

Though I didn't agree with the archaic views of the community, I had to respect them as long as I was here.

"Mr. Glicks," Turner said.

"You may go home. I'll see to my daughter."

Turner glanced my way and I gave him a tiny nod that I'd be fine. He then nodded to my father and headed out, not in the direction of his family home. I wondered if he was headed to see Margaret, the woman I'd seen him with the last time I'd been home.

"You need to leave that boy alone," my father directed.

"I'm not—"

He didn't give me a chance to finish. "He's a good boy and deserves better."

As much as I wanted to believe I wasn't that girl who needed her father's approval, it stung to hear him say that. I opened my mouth to protest, but he was right. Turner did deserve better and not because I was bad. But because if nothing else, this moment put in complete clarity how much I no longer belonged here.

"Why are you here?" he asked as if I wasn't welcomed.

His voice held no amusement nor his face a smile, but it wasn't anger that fueled his words. My father, one of the leaders of our community, was tasked with the wellbeing of our sanctuary. My showing up without warning after I'd fled so long ago could only mean one thing to him. Trouble.

Most children could be honest with their parents. But if I told him everything, I wouldn't be welcomed. Though I hadn't completely let myself think about it, the black roses Lizzy said had been sent to me bothered me. Who would have sent such a thing and why?

Then there had been all of those warning messages I'd received. I wanted to believe they had to do with the women in Scott or Kalen's lives. But what if they had something to do with the fraud I'd uncovered at King Enterprises?

"I've asked you a question," Father repeated.

"I missed home," which wasn't a lie.

He held my gaze, gauging my truthfulness.

"Your presence confuses your sisters." I wasn't surprised he didn't mention my brothers. As men in general, they were held to different standards. "You will keep your answers to their questions about the outside world to a minimum. Your sisters are coming of age and you don't want to affect a potential advantageous pairing for them."

If my father hadn't been the man he was, I would want to take my sisters far away. But though Father was firm about a man's role, he'd never been one to take choices away from his daughters. Otherwise, I wouldn't have been allowed to leave to go to college.

"Yes, Father."

"I assume your stay will be short. As it's late, you can make a pallet for yourself in the main room of the house. Tomorrow, however, you will see if Mary or Violet will take you in."

It hurt to hear that I wasn't welcomed, despite staying with one of my sisters would likely be more comfortable as they would have more space.

Though my spine was ramrod straight, I still gave him the respectful, "Yes, Father."

"You will also stay away from Turner. Margaret is so looking forward to a spring wedding, and I don't want you to be the cause of her disappointment."

Thankfully, the gasp of shock got stuck in my throat and I managed to dislodge another, "Yes, Father."

No hugs or questions regarding my wellbeing, he simply nodded and headed toward home. Not that I expected more. He simply wasn't that type of guy.

The main reason I followed like a dutiful daughter and didn't go to my car and leave was the chance of seeing my mother and siblings.

If my last few weeks had taught me anything, I'd learned the power of words. When to use them and when to say nothing. Kalen had the art down. Now was the time to hold my tongue. I could always leave. It would take a great deal of strength on my part to stay.

As I followed, I tried to believe my father still loved me, but he hadn't given me any indication that he did. It was my mother who loved me unconditionally. She'd proven that when she'd used her words to fight for my right to leave. Though honestly, I would have bet my father was somewhat relieved at my decision to go. Yet, I was back without prior approval, which appeared to have my father on edge.

When we reached home, firelight glowed in the windows. I stayed on the porch for a minute after my father walked in before entering my childhood home.

I didn't have to look far for my mother in our tiny four-room house. She waited for me at the dining room table, which was in what was called our great room. It was the main area that included what could traditionally be called a living room-kitchen combo in the secular world. The other three rooms were my parents', the boys', and the girls' bedrooms.

The only light came from the fire in the hearth and the candles on the table. Even if I hadn't been there earlier, I wouldn't have needed the light to remember what this place looked like. Built by my father's hands and other members of the community, it was still solid and functional as the first day they'd moved in. Everything had its place. As sparse as it was, it was homey and more inviting than Lizzy's parents' posh apartment.

The timber used to build this place was kept natural, free of paint inside and out. The floors and ceiling boasted the same. A wood-burning oven was positioned on one side of the house and the hearth on the other. We didn't have a refrigerator because our house held no electricity. We did have an icebox, which literally meant that a block of ice was used to keep the space cold. A few cupboards and a small worktable made up the rest of the tiny kitchen.

Two long *sofas* were fashioned from wood with hand-made cushions set across from each other. The hearth created division between them. In the middle of the two *rooms* was the long table worn with loving nicks when as kids we played games and from accidental flicks of forks and knives. There at the end of the long table, perched like a king because he was head of the household, my father now sat.

He steepled his hands, the tips grazing his long fiery beard. Mother sat to his left. Her dark locks muted by time. Even in the candlelight, I could see time had been kind to them.

"Sit, Bailey," my father commanded. I just complied. His instruction was always to be followed no matter what.

I sat across from my mother, meeting her subdued smile.

"Your mother very much wants to know how you've been."

This was the test. He wanted to see how I'd answer these questions that would come up here at home and in the community. I understood my role not to poison anyone, including my mother, about a grand life outside of our town if one could call it that.

Looking into my mother's earnest face, I knew I couldn't be completely dishonest.

"Everything's fine. I've been busy with an audit. Things didn't go as planned and I had an opportunity to take some time for myself," I said.

Mother reached over and covered my hand with hers. "I'm sorry for that, but I'm glad you're here. Is your fiancé okay with you being gone?"

Of course, she'd think of that. I glanced away and muttered, "That didn't work out either."

"What did you do this time?" Father asked as if exasperated.

"What did I do?" I spat, keeping my voice low as to not disturb my younger siblings who were down for the night. "I said yes to the wrong man who couldn't keep his hands to himself."

"Is that a surprise?" he challenged. "Men like Scott Hayes, without faith, whose lives revolve around money, have no honor."

It wasn't a surprise to hear him recite my ex's given name, as I'd written to my mother with the news of our engagement.

I almost laughed at the hypocrisy but managed to keep myself in check.

"I guess I would have been better off here, subservient to some man, spitting out babies as he decided whether or not one wife was enough," I gritted out, unable to keep my mouth shut.

Everything went silent. Mother looked as though she held her breath, waiting for what my father would do next.

He didn't even look mad. Calmly, he said, "You were never subservient, Bailey. From the moment you were born, you lived to defy me. As soon as you were able to walk, if I said go left, you would go right. None of your brothers or sisters ever dared to cross me, except you."

"Is that why you hate me?" I asked, my voice trembling against my wishes.

When he didn't answer, I almost got up. In a final act of some semblance of respect, I said, "May I be excused?" Though the words felt like lava in my throat.

My father pushed away from the table and stood,

towering over us, making the point of who was in charge. "As I mentioned before, it's best you not stay here after tonight."

"Jacob," my mother admonished, curling her hand around his forearm, trying to stop his edict.

"Catelyn," my father said. His voice was softer yet still firm with her. "She can stay with Marigold."

My mother sighed and nodded her head. Marigold, or rather Mary as the siblings called her, was my younger sister only by a year. "She has space. It's just her, Thomas, and the baby," she said to me.

But she hadn't forgotten my earlier request and glanced at Father who nodded. But I waited for the words.

"Yes, you may be excused," she said, sounding as sad and resigned to be stuck in the middle between father and daughter as she had when I'd lived here.

There weren't any choices for privacy. Despite the cold, I set out into the cover of darkness that completely obliterated any light.

I wrapped my arms around myself to ward off the chill as snow still lightly fell. When the door opened, I wasn't surprised to see my mother wrapped in an afghan.

She came over and cupped my cheeks.

"Let me look at you. Still as pretty as the day you were born."

The love in her eyes broke me. "Mom," I said, choking out a sob.

She wrapped me in a loving embrace. One that I hadn't known I needed until I was there. Fiercely, I hugged her back and let the tears I'd been holding in fall.

She rubbed circles on my back, and for the first time all day, I felt completely safe.

"He's not mad at you," she began.

"Of course, he is. I'm his one failure."

She pulled back and met my eyes. "You are not. He's scared for you. You're out there in the world where he can't keep you safe."

That's when it hit me. "How did Dad know Scott comes from money?"

I hadn't mentioned that in my letter to them, knowing Father's feelings.

Her eyebrow lifted. "Your father may not be much for technology, but he knows how to search. He found an article about Scott and his family."

He could have only found something in the society section. I couldn't imagine my father reading about social events where dressing the part would be more important than the reason for the event.

I imagined Scott's parents had orchestrated getting themselves in such an article likely in *The New York Times*.

Unable to imagine my father doing a google search on me, I said as much.

"He might not say it, but he's very proud of you. He's just an old-fashioned man who wants to know the man you're with is worthy of you."

I wanted to believe her, but she saw the best in him as he always pointed out the worst in me.

"Now, come inside and tell me about this man."

I stopped and glared at her.

She smiled. "Come on now. I see that look. Someone has broken your heart and it's most certainly not Scott."

She made it very hard to keep secrets from her. "Father?" I asked before following her inside.

"You know he has an early start. He'll be in bed. We'll have the fire to ourselves to gossip."

She winked and I gave her a wry smile. We sat by the fire, and though I'd wanted desperately to forget about the man who'd crawled into the depths of my emotions, I whispered the story, an edited version.

"He lied to me," I said, in conclusion. "His name wasn't Kalen Brinner, but Jeremy King."

"Wasn't it, though," she said. "Kalen Brinner is also a part of his name, correct?"

I shrugged. "He claimed as much, but that isn't the point."

"Isn't it? We all have secrets. My parents had them when they moved here for a better life, or so they said. Yet the community embraced us and made us feel welcome."

"But you didn't want to be here."

She shook her head with a secretive smile. "I hated every second."

"Until Father?"

She sighed. "Until your father," she agreed, with a girlish smile on her face. "His courting was so subtle; I had no idea it was happening. He was so sweet, showing me the beautiful life we could have together."

It seemed foreign to hear that about the man who seemed so cold and remote.

"He's a good man," she added. "Sometimes love can be found in the oddest of places."

I thought about the gorgeous but grumpy Scottish man who had stormed into my life.

"He doesn't love me."

"But you him?" she asked.

I shrugged, not ready to admit anything yet. "It doesn't matter. It's over."

She didn't press, just patted the hands I'd rested in my lap. "Let me get you some blankets."

She stood after pressing a kiss to the top of my head. "Maybe he isn't the one. Maybe Turner is."

Before I could respond, she'd disappeared behind her bedroom door.

I closed my eyes and let myself think of the possibilities. Could I live here in this community for the rest of my life? Could I do that as Turner's wife?

EIGHT

KALEN

THE PHONE FELT IT MIGHT CRACK UNDER THE pressure of my grip. It took several calming moments before I was able to place it on my desk without slamming it. It wasn't conceivable to me that every muscle in my body could be so tense at the same time. My chest felt constricted, like it was impossible to get enough air.

Bailey had vanished, at least on paper. She'd rented a car and Griffin was working to track its GPS. But hacking the car rental company's records wasn't proving easy, and not because they had great security. Their records were a mess even online. It wasn't a simple search for Bailey's name. He had to search by car, and without knowing what car she rented, he had to go one by one.

The thought of spanking that sexy little ass of hers for making me worry about her had me gripping my cock.

Fuck. I squeezed a little harder in hopes pain would kill the erection that sprang to life at the thought of her.

All the blood in my body rushed to my dick, imagining her spread eagle on my desk. That's how our last encounter should have gone, not with her saying goodbye as if it were for the last time.

It was that frustration that pushed past any fantasies I had. I pinched above my brow, hoping to stave off a headache. Why couldn't I let this woman go?

It had only been a couple of days since I had her.

"Mr. King."

I looked up to see the administrative temp entering my office. My steadfast assistant called out sick for the first time since she'd been in my employ. She also made sure I wouldn't be without help and had arranged a short-term replacement.

"I'm sorry to bother you, but you didn't answer your line. I was concerned something might be wrong."

Red hair capped a cute face. No, that wasn't true. Her hair was nothing like Bailey's. It was more of a strawberry blonde that topped a petite package. I didn't have to glance up far to notice her blouse was unbuttoned a little too far.

"I'm fine," I managed to say and not sound on the edge like I was.

She continued forward like there was more she wanted to say. "Okay," she uttered. Her skirt rose higher than mid-thigh as she moved and was almost inappropriate for the office. There was an offer in her stroll toward me, but I didn't have to take the bait. I found the temp's eyes again, only to see the *come fuck me* in them.

"I just wanted to say what an honor it is to work for you today." There was a sway in her hips she wanted me to notice. I knew better. I was aware of women who wanted me. Most of them tended to get a little clingy when the deed was done. My plan had always been never to get involved with anyone, not here in the States. *Keep your eye on the prize*, I'd told myself. I wanted to go back to Scotland. My life was there.

"You have a meeting at two," she said, prowling toward me.

I shifted my gaze from her to my computer screen to remind myself what that appointment was all about.

The temp, however, wasn't giving up. "I know you haven't had lunch."

I glanced up again to see that she was a meter or two from my desk. I kept my gaze on her face to keep things professional.

"I could bring something in and have it spread before you," she said in a sultry way that was dialed up to the max.

She ended that statement with a wink, making an innuendo too glaring to overlook. She'd either realized her mistake of what sounded like an offer or she was shy about making it. Either way, she'd turned pink, highlighting the freckles that swept over her nose.

There was a decision to be made. She didn't work for me directly and never would. I would ensure that. I had no plans of ever replacing my current assistant.

But Bailey was gone. She'd made it painfully clear where her head was. And when had I ever chased a woman?

Could my father actually be right for once? The best thing for my plans and the future of this company would be to let her go.

There was a definite way to try to forget her.

I heard myself say, "What exactly are you offering?"

NINE

Lass, he called out to me from the hazy backdrop of my bedroom. I tried to remember Lizzy's house wasn't soundproofed as Kalen kissed his way up the curve of my arm. I pressed my lips closed to hold in a moan as I squirmed a bit under his ministrations. Wanting so much more, I wiggled my bottom against his huge erection, hoping to tease him into action as I lay on my side.

No need to rush, lass. I promise to get you there more than once, he said, coming ever closer to my mouth, teasing me with the promise of his kiss, which I craved far more than I ever thought possible.

He cupped my breast, squeezing just shy of pain while rubbing a thumb back and forth over the taut nipple. The sensations were like a lit match dropping into gasoline. Every inch of my skin sparked to life.

Never will I let you go, he commanded. His lips changed directions just as he maneuvered me from my side to my back.

In the stillness of the night, he hovered over me with his

large body. His green eyes peered into my soul like he'd eat me alive.

With expert hands, he pushed my thighs apart and swiped his tongue down my slit. My back bowed as if wanting to deliver a Cupid's arrow straight from my heart and into his.

This man... he worked my body into such a frenzy, feasting on me as if I tasted of milk and honey.

I want more, I nearly called out. I was so close, I could taste it.

"Bailey."

The voice destroyed my illusions like a wrecking ball into the side of a building.

I blinked away the dreams of Kalen that had kept my brain active through the night. His touch may have been a memory, but it was one reluctant to be forgotten.

What was more disturbing was finding my hand on my center as my father walked out of his bedroom into the room. Never had I been more grateful for the blankets that still covered me.

On a yawn, quickly I discreetly shifted my hand away from bringing the reality of my fantasies to life before my father made it over to lord over me.

The sky had barely begun to lighten through the windows when Father's command rang out.

"Have a care and make yourself useful."

Father wouldn't accept a nod, so I said, "Yes, Father," without a second of hesitation.

His glare of disdain could have meant he'd heard any noises I'd made while in the throes of sleep or Mother's belief that he loved me was wrong. I thought the latter. He didn't care about me at all. I ignored both options to allay any embarrassment and so I wouldn't begin to hate the man.

After he left out the door, I got to my feet and got ready for the day.

I lovingly folded the hand knit afghans my mother made that had kept me warm and placed them back over the side of the sofas. A plate of fruit and cheese rested on the table. Things weren't left out by mistake. You would be inviting critters of all kinds to break bread with you if they got wind of it. Thus, I knew my mother left the food for me.

The growl in my tummy was persistent, but not as much as the pressure in my bladder. I walked out the back door and several yards to the wooden structure. Opening the door, I appreciated my family's use of natural bacteria and other things sprinkled down the hole that rested beneath the seat. It broke down the waste left behind, keeping the smell to a dull yuck. It was almost odd to find a roll of toilet paper in such a place that felt so foreign after a few years gone by. Some conveniences were still used even though invented in modern times.

The chill was what had me hurrying to complete my task.

When walking back, I caught sight of the shower stall that was attached to the back of the house where a well pump stood. But it was too cold for such a thing. Water warmed by fire would be used for bathing until the weather once again permitted outdoor showers.

Our house did boast one extra tiny room in the house. It held a tub. I believe it was a gift from my father to my mother when he built the place. However, with no indoor plumbing, it was a pain to use. Buckets of hot water had to be brought in to fill it.

Yet, I eased back into the life I'd been born in as easy as riding a bike after you learned. Some things you never forgot. So, once I was ready for the day, I followed the women making their way to the community epicenter, ready to get an assigned task for the day. I ignored the stares and whispers, as there would be many.

By mid-afternoon, Turner found me in the designated area inside the center using a laundry bucket to rub my sisters' dresses against a washboard. The day was warmer with the sunlight streaming through the windows and the hearth blazing with fire.

My aching arms had forgotten such manual use. I wanted to sink into the washbasin and douse myself with the water. I was working on the last dress and craved a bath before my family got home from their chores of the day.

Holding my hand up to block the sunlight streaming through the window, I looked up at Turner. His eyes were a burnished gold in the morning light. Their blaze was squarely on me.

"I thought you might be hungry," he said in a matter-of-fact voice.

His lips were quirked, his hair sexily tousled on his head. I glanced away, not wanting to fall under his spell like I'd done as a girl.

My gaze landed on the picnic basket he carried. Getting to my feet, I wrung out the last of the dresses and strolled over to the indoor clothesline. Pinning the garment, I let my shoulders sag as my arms felt as if they couldn't carry one more thing.

"I don't know what to say."

"Thank you," he said simply.

It wasn't that easy. I'd seen him earlier with Margaret.

"Let's take a walk," he said softly.

I could feel eyes on us, so I hustled out the side door of the center and into the chill of the mid-winter morning.

Golden fields of dormant crops were dusted lightly with remnants of yesterday's snowfall. Beyond it was my family home, which was on the outskirts of town closer to the entrance. Our family's primary means of contribution to the community was farming. It was our primary business and brought much-needed revenue to the community to pay government taxes and buy supplies and goods we couldn't harvest, grow, or obtain lawfully from our own lands. However, my parents weren't there.

They were most likely in the building where we kept harvested goods left over from the market times and prepared to keep for the winter.

Dead on my feet, I let Turner drag me across the land toward the creek. On the spot we'd spent the day before, we sat on a spread quilt, and he pulled out meat and bread after starting a fire.

"Do you think that was wise?" I finally asked as his fingers offered me a nibble of meat.

"What?" he said with a smirk that meant he knew exactly what I was talking about.

"For everyone to see us together?"

Before I said more, I accepted the tender meat that burst with flavor inside my mouth.

"I'm not married, and neither are you."

He spoke so easily as if we didn't live in a compound with rules that dated back to the eighteenth century.

I thought about my father's warnings far too late. "Aren't you courting Margaret?"

"I'm not in love with Margaret."

He hadn't exactly answered, and I wasn't completely sure how I felt about it.

"Is she in love with you?"

He shrugged. "I've never lied to her. I would have married her a few years ago if I wanted that and she knows it."

His hand came up with another offering, and with the absence of a response I took it. The bread was slightly sweet but rich and buttery too. My tongue accidently snaked across his fingers as he glided them out of my mouth. His eyes met mine and I could feel his burning gaze. As much as I hated it, Kalen continued to hover in the back of my mind.

To break the tension, I asked, "Who cooked this?"

With a wolfish grin, Turner said, "I did."

That surprised me. "Since when did you become such a great cook?" The Turner I knew was treated like a king as were all the males in his family. Thus, cooking had never been his chore.

"Since becoming a bachelor."

Because I was one of the reasons he still remained unmarried, it made the moment awkward.

"It's okay, Bails."

I didn't want to rehash one of my not-so finer moments. Yet, I found myself repeating what I told him the day before, "I was afraid you'd ask me to stay."

With patient eyes, he watched me for a second. "Would

you do it again?"

It was a good question. Had spending over three years of my life in a wasted relationship with Scott been worth it? I hadn't really loved him. I stayed with him out of some sense of duty and honor to my family for my perceived sins. Then again, had I not been with Scott, I may have never met Kalen that fateful night. Would I go back and stay with Turner?

"No, not the same way," I said honestly. "I never wanted to hurt you."

I read into his half-smile that he didn't entirely believe me. But he reached into the basket to pull something else out. Out came a palm-sized strawberry tart, my favorite. Delight filled me. I hadn't had one of these in ages. "Your mother?"

He nodded, and I took the proffered dessert from his hand with relish. I bit into it like a woman possessed. It tasted like heaven. And I might have moaned out loud, because Turner laughed.

"There are more," he teased.

I slapped at his arm playfully, careful not to drop the last bit of tart. "These are the absolute best."

It was true. The woman was gifted with baked goods. They were French bakery worthy according to my tongue despite the fact the strawberries weren't fresh but from preserves.

Somewhere in the middle of lunch, we found that casualness between us. It was easy to be friends again, transported to a time and place when we had no cares about our future.

For the second day in a row, I sat close to a man I would

always love. The question was if I was still *in love* with him. As much as I wanted to be, how easy it would make my life, Kalen snuck in my head like a stealer of my heart. I needed those feelings to go away, and fast. The way Turner looked at me, he would be asking the question about the idea of us far sooner than I would be ready to answer.

There was a moment when I thought Turner might kiss me, but footfalls had us both looking up.

"Why am I not surprised to find you here?"

Again, I felt like I was twelve as I always did around my father.

"I asked her here, sir," Turner said, standing up for me.

"Yet she knows better," Father chastised.

Turner went to speak, but I held up a hand to stop him. My future in the community was certain. I would never be accepted back, not that I wanted to be. Turner, on the other hand, still had a choice.

"Thank you for lunch, Turner. But Father is right. I should go."

I got to my feet and ignored Turner's questioning stare. He didn't want me to leave and had gone as far as to reach for me, but I moved just far enough so he couldn't touch me.

"I'm sure they are looking for you," Father said to Turner.

You could take the girl out of the simple life, but you couldn't take the simple life out of the girl. Before I could think, I said, "I'll clean this up."

Turner glared at me. "I can do it," he said, slicing the air with his statement.

I straightened, feeling caught in two worlds, but this ground belonged to one.

"Let's go, girl," Father commanded.

And like a soldier in my father's army, I followed.

Once we were out of the trees and back into the clearing of farmland, he pressed me with a glower that would stop a raging bull. Immediately, any thoughts of what I might say in my own defense halted.

"Tonight is the monthly council meeting," he said. "As long as you are here, you might as well be an asset to this community. Use that fancy degree we paid for and prepare the books for an accounting at sundown."

It would have been easy to mention that scholarships and grants had funded most of my college. And I could have asked why the current bookkeeper hadn't prepared for this meeting, as she surely was fully aware of the schedule and duties in my stead. In fact, I'd only taken over for her after she apprenticed me. Once I left, the duty fell back on her as she served double duty as school mistress and bookkeeper.

However, none of that mattered. My father had spoken. There was no choice for me other than to comply. I didn't resent it because I'd come here and knew what my responsibilities would be. I was eating the community's food and would be using other supplies. It was everyone's responsibility to contribute however they could. So I nodded, and my father stalked off toward the center of town.

I stood for only another minute in time to see Turner come through the brush. So much hadn't been said. When our eyes met, there were questions in his gaze I ignored. Instead, I found myself twisting the ring on my finger before I turned from him and headed in the direction of the schoolhouse. As I walked, the damnable Kalen crept back into my thoughts.

TEN

KALEN

GRIFFIN HAD JUST FINISHED GIVING ME THE NEWS.

"The community is in the middle of nowhere for the most part," he said.

"But is she safe?"

"As safe as anyone." His brow rose. "I'm beginning to think this one means more to you than you've admitted."

"I've caused her problems," I snapped, glaring at him.

"You haven't received any threats. This may not have anything to do with you. Besides, she's out of New York. You should be relieved."

"I'm not. We don't know for sure who's targeting her and why."

"Are you in love with her?" he asked pointedly, taking me aback.

"In love with whom?"

Both Griffin and I looked up and watched as Connor strode in as the question left his tongue.

"Who let you in?" I asked, annoyed by the interruption, though Griffin's question was also to blame.

"You gave me a key," he said, holding the black card up that would give him access to the private elevator to my apartment.

"What brings you by?"

"Dad sent me to make sure you don't back out tonight."

I leaned back in my desk chair and steepled my fingers. So much had happened today, I'd forgotten.

"You forgot?" he asked, pulling the words from my head.

"I've been busy."

"With your new assistant." His added smirk was irritating.

"She's not new. She was temporary. But how would you know that? You don't even work there."

Connor did spend an awful lot of time in the company offices for someone who reportedly didn't want anything to do with the business.

"I have my spies," he said.

A quick glance at Griffin and I didn't have to say more. I trusted my brother, but I couldn't ignore that he could potentially be the person behind an orchestrated attempt at my downfall.

"Besides, she's making noise with Human Resources about you letting her go. Though everyone including God knows you wouldn't have to resort to sexual harassment to get a woman in bed."

I blew out a breath. "I guess it's a good thing I engaged the recorder when she came into my office."

Connor might have responded if not for my son who ran into my home office.

"Uncle Connor," he yelled and wrapped himself

around my brother's leg. Connor scooped him up. "Are you eating with us?"

Connor looked at me and I said, "If he wants to."

"What are we having?" he asked Gabe.

Gabe rattled off the menu.

"Absolutely," Connor said to my son before setting him back on his feet.

When he smiled at my brother, I felt the familial bonds tug at me, something I didn't have growing up.

Gabe ran over to me and climbed in my lap.

"Are we making deals?" Gabe asked me.

Griffin laughed. "Like father, like son."

"We're making dollars," Gabe said proudly before glancing back at me. "Or is it pounds?"

I smiled. This boy was my entire world. "Both. All money is good."

"But Scottish money is best," my son announced.

"Aye."

"Aye, aye," Griffin agreed.

That might not technically be true, but I wanted my son to be proud of his heritage.

Connor chimed in, "You do know your da is American, right?"

Gabe looked at me for confirmation. "I told you I was born here," I said.

"But Grandma is Scottish, right?" I nodded. "And you're Scottish?" he asked Griffin.

"Born and bred," Griffin answered.

"And you're American, Uncle Connor?"

"Yes, but my mom is Irish."

"Irish?" Gabe asked, his nose wrinkling. "We're better at football, right, Da?"

Elspeth, my son's nanny, came in. "Dinner is ready. Come, Gabe, and wash yer hands."

Gabe scooted off my lap and followed Elspeth out.

A few seconds later, Connor spoke up. "Did I ever mention how hot she is?"

"Leave her be, Connor. She's had enough trouble in her life without having to deal with the likes of you."

Connor acted pained. "I would never."

"Those three words have never been true out of your mouth."

Griffin laughed. "Leave the lass alone."

Connor shrugged. "Back to why I'm here. Dad is expecting you. With everything going on, he expects you to be there."

My time in the shadows had come to an end. It had been decided for me to make a very public appearance. My father had even chosen my date for the evening. I was never more grateful that Bailey was home. A place that didn't have TVs and such. Maybe she wouldn't find out about my night out before I had a chance to explain.

ELEVEN

My stomach continued its warpath as I made my way to the square after working on the books that afternoon. It was potluck night on council meeting nights. On these occasions the food would be plentiful. Every family brought at least one dish. There would be more than enough to choose from. Dinner would be served in the town hall.

Spotting my father, I headed in his direction with a folder of the information he needed to start the elders' meeting. The sun was just visible on the horizon. Thankfully, I wasn't late. When he spotted me, it was the first time since I arrived back home I saw approval on his face.

Before I could reach him, I was stopped by Turner stepping into my path. He didn't know that I needed to get this information into my father's hands before I could breathe again. The need to please Father was like a pressing weight I didn't think I'd ever overcome.

"We need to talk," Turner insisted. He didn't give me time to answer. "Because it feels like you're going to run again."

"No," I said softly, closing my eyes to the emotion that hit me every time I was near him. "I just have to get these numbers to my father." I raised the folder as proof.

He ran a hand through his brown hair and nodded before he stepped out of my way. I gave Turner a smile before I found a scowl on my father's face. I sighed, because I was starting to wonder if a hotel would have been a better hiding place than coming home.

"Here," I said to my father, handing him the ledger.

"Remember, everything you do, doesn't just reflect on you, but the whole family."

"I know, but Father—"

He halted like he'd been ready to bolt.

"I need to use the computer."

The computer was locked away in the offices on the second floor of the community center.

His eyes narrowed on me.

"I need to check on word from my job in case they need something from me."

The real reason was I wondered if official word had come through about my future as an employee.

He reached into his pocket and handed me the keys. With that, he marched off like he couldn't stand to be in my presence. I sighed, feeling trapped between two worlds.

I headed there straightaway. After logging in to my email, I found I had two. The first was the formal letter from Human Resources placing me on leave. The second was from Kalen. There were two lines.

Where are you, lass? We need to talk.

My reply was simple and consisted of three words. ***No, we don't.***

Thankfully, I didn't have time to be rattled. I was pulled into a yawn worthy elders' meeting to give a verbal accounting of the books as soon as I exited the small computer room. There were a lot of nods and several questions. Luckily, I'd spent the night before going through the ledgers and could answer most of their questions. That had been a stroke of luck. After I had been sent away, my father gave me strict instructions to help the other women in the food line, dishing out plates after I returned the keys.

The chattering women were more than happy to put me to work.

My mother smiled and commented, "You look a little thin," while others looked curious.

The only response I offered was to hold up the plate I was adding a side dish to. With a waiting line, no one had time to comment more or ask about my reappearance in town.

My feet felt like weighted blocks were attached to them by the time everyone had been served. Finally, I was able to make my own plate and head to the table where my older sister Violet sat with an unfamiliar man.

Seated at the end of a long table, they were curiously left with plenty of seats in between them and another group who sat at the other end. She was all but isolated with only the man who I assumed was her husband.

Violet and I had always been close. She was a free spirit much as I had been. When I suggested she should go off to college with me, she'd only rolled her eyes and told me that the only thing she'd ever be good at was mothering. So it had been a surprise when it was Mary who had given birth first. In fact, Mary was also the first of us to get married.

"Vi." I quickly set my plate down and then hugged her.

"Bails," she cried out with genuine excitement.

After returning from the elders' meeting, there hadn't been time for me to greet her before I was put to work. She'd had a plate and had been talking to various people.

The man sitting across from her turned and I got the full impact of him. He had the kind of face that belonged on magazines. And for a second, I tried to place him.

"Bails, this is Steven, my husband. Steven, this is my younger sister, Bailey."

He reached out a hand, revealing hints of tattoos just above his tunic neckline and peeking around his wrist. His long, dirty blond hair was tied back. His beard was slightly unruly but in that appealing way most women found attractive.

"Bailey, I like. It's a pretty cool name."

If I hadn't known everyone in town, I certainly would have guessed from the casual way he spoke, he was an outsider.

"Thanks."

Violet chimed in. "We're all named after flowers," she said and began to name us off like her husband hadn't met them. "There's me, then Bailey, which is a flower name, Mary, but her name is actually Marigold, Rose, and Poppy."

"Yeah," he said. "I hadn't really thought about it when I met them."

I found it extremely odd it had never come up in

conversation with a man she'd married, but kept that to myself.

Even odder was that strangers weren't welcomed easily as residents in our community. Our leaders were cautious of those who might place themselves among our ranks to get insider information to write or publish stories to confirm the outside world's beliefs that we were some sort of cult or to exploit us in articles or postings on social media.

You had to prove yourself to be allowed to join our clan. He'd obviously passed my father's test since he'd been allowed to marry my sister. So I gave him a measure of trust.

"It's nice to meet you, Steven."

"It's probably cramped at your parents' house. You're welcome to stay with us," he offered.

I glanced at Vi, who smiled like the world shined on her.

"I'm supposed to stay at Mary's. Speaking of, I'm not sure when they go to bed for the night. With a new baby, I don't want to intrude on their schedule. It would be best if I head on over after helping clean up. I don't want to arrive late and wake them."

Violet brightened. "Don't stay with her. You're welcome to stay with us."

"We have more than enough room at our place," Steven added, with a hearty smile.

I liked him. There was something easygoing about him. Didn't mean I wasn't curious about how he ended up here.

"Okay... I'll stay with you tonight. I should go find Mary and let her know."

I hugged Vi one more time and waved to her husband. Before I could leave, my younger sisters, whom I had only glanced at while they slept, found me. They hugged both

Violet and me as if they'd seen neither of us in a very long time.

Two of my brothers, however, hadn't bothered to greet me except to say "Hi" in the food line as if it hadn't been years since I'd seen them. Jacob, the older at seventeen, carried himself like my father, regal and sure of himself. John, the younger at fourteen, seemed in awe of his big brother but was more reserved and shy.

He'd given me a winning smile. I was sure he would have happily hugged me if not for Jacob at his side. So when my sisters walked away, I sought out not only Mary, but my brothers too. I found the boys first.

"John," I said, enveloping him in a hug. "I missed you."

He squeezed me back. When he spoke, his voice lacked the baritone that came with age and, in fact, cracked a little. "Bails." A shyness that screamed embarrassment crossed his face. I wanted to tell him he wouldn't be the squeaky boy for long. Yet, I held my tongue.

When Jacob walked over, trying to be cool and lightly punched me on my shoulder, I took him by surprise in my embrace. "Hey, Jake," I teased. He was Jake and Father was Jacob. It had always been that way to keep them separate since they shared a name.

"Bails," he hesitantly said, patting my back awkwardly before pulling away. "Yeah, since you're so happy to see us, maybe you could do us a favor."

"And what's that?" I asked, raising my eyebrows.

"There's a dance Friday. Father won't let us go unless we have an escort." He rolled his eyes like it was nonsense.

An arm at my shoulder acknowledged the presence of Turner at my side. "She'll come because she's my date."

John glanced back and forth between us, and Jake got a wicked gleam in his eyes. "I bet she is," Jake said before striding off. Apparently, he was done with me. The strawberry blonde in the corner he was heading toward was all the confirmation I needed that I'd been sorely dismissed. John smiled before following in his brother's wake.

"Date," I said, swiveling to face Turner.

"Yeah, the one I was going to ask you on. But thankfully, Jake took care of that."

I almost contradicted him when the elders strolled in. Everything quieted and I headed back to my place by Violet with Turner in tow.

The meeting only brought me farther back in time. It was almost as if I'd never left. According to the elders, things were good. They talked about the plans for surviving winter and preparing for spring.

After the meeting was over, it was up to the younger generation to remove any plates or trash left on the tables. The women were huddled to the side in front of large basins either washing or drying the dishes, while others wrapped up leftover food for those who had iceboxes and wanted to take it.

The men worked together to move the large tables and benches to one side of the hall, leaving the place empty for whatever events were to come. And according to Jake, that would most likely be a dance on Friday night.

When it was all done, I went to find Mary.

I found her with a gaggle of females as she held her baby close to her chest.

"Can I speak with you?"

She rolled her eyes, which got a lot of giggles from the

peanut gallery. I ignored it because you couldn't choose family. And though she may have hated me, I still loved my sister.

"What is it that you want now?" she asked, sounding put out.

"I'm staying with Vi tonight."

"Of course, you are, after all the trouble I went through to make a place for you to sleep."

My father must have talked to her before I could and warned her of my arrival.

"I'm sorry. I can cancel."

She waved me off with her free hand. "It's better this way. You won't disturb my routine. I was only doing it as a favor to Father."

"Right," I said, trying to bite my tongue. "Far be it for me to interfere in your life."

I walked away and tried to see it from Mary's point of view and couldn't.

By the time I made it back to Vi, her husband wasn't anywhere to be seen.

"Can I walk you ladies home?"

Vi looked up at Turner with dreamy eyes. Of course, she'd crushed on him. Turner was closer to her age than he was to mine. Being the good-natured person she was, when she found out years ago that Turner and I had eyes for each other outside of friendship, she'd bowed out and told me I was a lucky girl.

On the other hand, Mary had taken it badly. She'd always competed with me at every turn. I wasn't even surprised at her choice of husband. Thomas had pursued me until he found out about my betrothal to Turner and backed off. Their wedding had been the reason I'd returned home a couple of years ago.

"We don't need your protection like we did when we were little," I teased him. Honestly, I wanted time to talk with my sister before we were near her husband.

"What kind of man would I be if I let two beautiful women walk home after dark alone?"

His chivalry was sweet, but I needed answers. I wrapped my arm around my sister and pulled ahead of Turner.

"Why didn't you tell me you were getting married?" I asked.

Her cheeks brightened. "It was kind of sudden."

I couldn't help but look down at her belly.

"No, silly. Steven needed a place to stay."

I stopped as warning bells rang in my head.

"How well do you know this guy?"

She gave me a patronizing smile. "Well enough. Trust me. I love him."

Still, I held my ground, prepared to demand answers.

She gazed up at Turner and then back to me. "We met at market. Several times."

I arched an eyebrow. There wasn't a lot of time to talk while working. Many pairs of eyes would be watching her at all times.

"We found a way," she said, answering questions I hadn't given voice to. "You should have seen him. He'd walk in and girls would surround him like he was some kind of music god."

"Rockstar," I corrected.

She nodded with her eyes glazed in that dreamy remembrance way.

"Yeah, like that. But he would seem to find *me* in the crowd."

Vi was beautiful but lacked confidence more than even me.

"Of course, he did."

"He courted me, like he knew our way. Notes and little gifts."

Gifts? I thought he needed a place to stay? But I didn't ask. Not yet at least.

"And when I found out he didn't have a place to live..." She shrugged.

"You married a guy so he could have somewhere to live," I repeated and realized too late how judgmental I sounded.

Her grin gone, she spoke with a flat tone. "It hasn't exactly been easy after you left."

I found the ground in search of a hole I could jump into. "I'm sorry."

She shook her head. "I don't blame you. It was nice that someone was interested in me. It wasn't like I had a ton of offers."

My father had been in talks with the Simon family for Violet to marry their eldest son before I left.

There was really only one other question that mattered. "Are you happy?"

Her frown immediately turned upside down, which was the answer. "Yes," she said. "I am."

I hugged her and took her hand. "Then let's go see your house."

The walk was long as my sister lived on the opposite edge of the community than our parents. The place was the same boxy construction as all the houses were. It was smaller than our parents', but clean.

"Can I offer you a beer?" Vi asked.

My eyes widened in shock, but Turner didn't seem surprised.

"You have beer?"

She shrugged. "Steven gets it."

"I'll have one," Turner said.

Vi went to the makeshift kitchen, lifting a hatch in the floor where her icebox would be. She pulled out a couple of beers and passed them out.

"Does anyone know about this?" I asked before removing the top.

"I know," Turner said and winked at me.

"Not everyone here is a Puritan, Bails," Vi said.

Soon enough Steven was back, and we talked a little. I learned that he was from Utah and grew up in a very conservative religious family until his mother moved to Pennsylvania when he was a teen.

I wanted to like him, but still I had questions.

My sister, a complete lightweight given that she wasn't a drinker, had become quite the chatterbox after only one beer. That is, until she turned her attention to her husband.

I took the cue to go outside, still nursing my beer. Being so far out, I didn't fear getting caught.

"I don't live far," Turner said, coming up behind me.

"Yeah." I glanced around. "I remember when this was just land."

"Not anymore."

Wistfully, I stared into the distance, ignoring the cold, but just soaking in the unencumbered land as the beer spread warmth throughout my body.

It took me a second to notice just how close Turner was. His eyes were on my mouth and I subconsciously licked my lips, feeling his heat.

"You know, you could always say you're staying with Violet, but stay with me instead."

And before I could answer, Turner tugged me closer.

TWELVE

KALEN

When my phone rang, I removed the hand wrapped around my bicep.

"Excuse me. I need to take this," I said to the woman whose red mouth pursed with annoyance at my escape.

I didn't wait for an answer. I headed for the patio doors despite the cold.

"What do you have?" I said by way of greeting.

Griffin's brusque answer was all about business.

"Someone entered her apartment." Just as I was about to ask if it was Lizzy, he said, "And not that hot blonde. Person was in all black with a hood pulled up."

"Body type?" I asked.

"Could be man or woman."

"Fuck. Do we know what they did?"

"They weren't in there long enough. I personally went by. They left a present."

"What was it?" I asked.

"Dead rat."

"What the hell does that mean?"

"Could be anything. I removed it."

"She's in danger," I said definitively.

"What's your call?" When I said nothing, Griffin added, "If you're too busy with the senator's daughter, we can talk about it tomorrow."

Just when I was about to set him straight, a hand slipped around my waist.

"It's cold out here. I know a place we could get warm."

There was a time when I would have taken her up on her offer. She'd made it clear earlier in the evening she wasn't looking for anything serious.

That had fit with my plans before Bailey had sauntered into my life. Now I took notice of all the sultry looks and offers that came my way. Something I hadn't done before.

"I can't," I said, surprising myself.

First, I'd sent the temp away and now this.

"Why not?" she said, shifting to stand before me. "I told you I'm just looking for fun."

"I'm not."

"And who's the lucky lady, and why isn't she here?"

Her glossy lips begged me to refute her, but I couldn't.

Bailey was in danger, the predator in me yelled. Every instinct in my body told me to go find and protect my woman.

"I have to go," I said, slipping out of her hold.

"You're missing out," she said, but didn't follow.

I went for my car, having made my obligatory appearance.

"Mr. King," someone called out as I exited the stately mansion owned by the senator.

I didn't turn back. "Do you have a response to the accusations that you're funneling money to offshore accounts for personal gain?"

I didn't answer but walked up to the valet to ask for my car. Instead of waiting, I followed.

Once I was behind the wheel, I called Griffin back.

"This is what I want to do," I began.

THIRTEEN

It felt almost sinful sitting out in the dark with Turner. When I'd lived here, that would have been a big *no-no*. And Turner was still one of the most handsome guys I'd ever laid eyes on. So why couldn't I just be with him? It was obvious he still held feelings for me. Kalen was a dream. Turner was a reality.

A sigh escaped me, and Turner came behind me and pulled my back to his chest.

"You know, I wasn't sure if I'd ever see you again."

I reached up and clutched at his arms because I was at a loss for words.

His chin rested on the top of my head.

"I'm glad you're here."

Still, I said nothing. My feelings were so twisted up.

"I'm still in love with you," he admitted.

I stopped everything, including breathing.

"Turner—"

"You don't have to say it back. I just needed you to know."

"I love you too." Though I'd been careful not to say *in love*. "But—"

"There's someone else," he finished.

I stepped out of his hold so I could turn and face him.

"There *was* someone else," I admitted.

"How serious is it?" he asked like I hadn't used the past tense.

"I ended things."

His frown lifted. "Then—"

"I'm not going to make that mistake again. When I left here, I was still in love with you. I jumped headfirst into a bad relationship with Scott because I needed the distraction to get over you. I'm still—"

"In love with this Scott?"

"Scott? No."

"Then who?"

There was a long pause as I considered how to answer. I wasn't ready to give voice to my feelings for Kalen.

"I'm not sure how I feel," I said instead. "But that's the point. I can't start things with you when I—"

"You don't know how you feel about him."

I couldn't answer that. I was determined not to feel a thing for Kalen. Instead, I said, "It wouldn't be fair to either of us."

He reached out and I let him take my hand.

"So let's take this slow. Go to the dance with me. Let me show you how good things can be."

I squeezed his hand. "I think maybe we should go alone." His face fell. "You need to figure things out with Margaret, and I need to figure things out with Kalen."

"That's his name?"

I nodded. "If there's any hope of an us, we need to be sure about the rest."

"I know what I want," he said.

"And if you did, Margaret wouldn't think she had a chance."

He pursed his lips, but stubbornly said, "Stay with me tonight and let me prove it to you."

I closed my eyes as memories of Turner and me wrapped up in each other filled my head, but they were quickly replaced with those of Kalen's demanding mouth covering every inch of me.

"We can't," I said and dropped his hand.

He bobbed his head. "Okay. I'll grant you time. It isn't like I haven't waited forever for you."

There was something a little sad in his expression and my heart clenched. I had no idea if I was doing the right thing. He was right there. All I had to do was walk away with him. But my feet remained rooted to the spot for a man I'd basically told to fuck off. For all I knew, he was with someone else.

FOURTEEN

A soft kiss to my neck and a warm body to my back made me squirm. "*Lass*, you've spoiled any chance of me getting a good night's sleep without your body next to mine."

His lips moved lower and forced a giggle from me. "You'll do just fine without me."

"Never," he declared. His brogue so thick, it rumbled from his chest into my back. "I'll never let you go, *lass*. You belong to me."

Lips kissed the nape of my neck and slowly slid down my spine.

"Put that pretty ass up in the air."

Needy, I compliantly did as he asked, getting to my knees.

Firm hands spread my legs and one eager finger submerged into my wet heat. I gasped, "Oh," on an exhaled moan.

He slid another finger inside. I felt fuller but nothing compared to his thick cock deep inside me. Preparing me for his penetration, he shoved in another and a cry left my lips.

"Are you ready for me, *lass*?"

"Yes," I breathed out.

It wasn't his shaft that penetrated me. A tongue flicked across my bundle of nerves, igniting the fire that only burned for him. His mouth covered my mound before his tongue sought entrance. He worked me stroke by stroke, effortlessly switching from finger to tongue and back again. His other hand found my breast and tweaked my nipple to a hardened peak.

The next time his tongue filled me, his finger found another entrance. My body tensed at the foreign sensation, but Kalen knew just what to do. He wasn't rough as he glided into me with precision.

"Yes, lass. You will love it. And soon, my cock will show you the pleasures here."

Just as I began to spasm, I reached for his thick black hair and found nothing. My eyes shot wide open. The memory still fresh in my mind.

Taking in my surroundings in the dark, I could only feel, not see very much. The fire had burned down, leaving less light than before. There was a warm body at my back along with a hand on my hip. Next came a kiss at my nape and said hand slipping down to my thigh.

"Bails," a whispered word, drawing me further out of dreamland. But the voice didn't belong to Kalen.

I rolled out of Turner's embrace and onto my side as I faced him. With distance between us, the fading light showed his expression held uncertainty.

It wasn't that I regretted his presence. We hadn't done

anything. It just felt dirty that I'd been dreaming about another man while in his arms.

Flashes of last night replayed in my mind. We'd gone back into the house and had another round of beers. We were all in various stages of inebriation. I'd invited Turner to stay. I hadn't wanted him walking home alone. There had been a slim chance of him getting caught, which seemed ridiculous, as we were adults.

"I'm sorry. I was dreaming." My hope was that my dream moans and cries hadn't spilled into my reality. If they had, hopefully he'd assumed they were for him. He said nothing in response, so I thought for sure I hadn't made a sound.

"Come here. I promise not to molest you in your sleep again unless you want me to," he teased.

A smile replaced my concern. I moved closer and allowed him to pull me into his solid arms. I closed my eyes again and hoped I wouldn't dream.

My eyes fluttered open to see daylight creep across the floor in a slim band of gold. What also stirred in the house below were voices.

"What's up with you and my baby sister?" I couldn't see Violet, but there was a long pause. Not feeling Turner at my back, I knew he was in the kitchen with her.

He didn't answer.

"I mean, she'd probably be really mad if she ever found out I had a thing for you."

It wasn't a declaration I hadn't already known.

"It's not like there are many great options around here. And I get it even if Mary didn't," Vi said before more pauses. "I mean, she was determined to have whatever

Bailey had. When you turned her down, she focused on the other boy that vied for Bail's attention and married Thomas."

"Mary's a determined girl." Turner's response was almost cold.

"That she is," my sister said. But Vi liked to talk and she continued. "Are you sure about this? I mean, you were pretty broken up after she left you. It's been a long time since I've seen you be yourself."

"I'm fine, and what happened between us should have never happened."

I froze. Something happened between him and Vi. I knew she crushed on him, but...

"I know. I'm rooting for you both. It's just, Bailey is never going to be satisfied staying here. And you, on the other hand, were made for this place, even though you are on your way out of the country. What are you going to do now?"

How often did my sister and Turner talk? And I couldn't get the question of what happened between the two of them out of my mind. It didn't surprise me that Mary betrayed me. But Violet? I never thought her capable, and a hurt deep inside me grew.

"I haven't yet told her my plans. She's not sure what she wants."

"That's what I'm saying." She didn't sound sure. "I don't want to see either of you hurt."

"Nothing's certain, but I hope she'll give us a chance."

It probably didn't say much that I sat there listening to their conversation, not that I'd meant to. Once I heard that something happened between the two of them, I was forced into silence. Somehow, I knew they may not ever tell me the truth of it willingly. However, it was time to stop spying. I got up and made a lot of noise.

When I stepped into the main room, Vi was there with a bright smile on her face. "Sleep well?"

"It was okay," I said and walked over to the stove to warm my hands. "Where is Steven?"

"He's already left for work duty."

I traded a sideways glance at Turner. "Wow, he's eager."

"He's trying to impress Father." She shrugged.

"He looks familiar," I said.

She brushed off that question. "Maybe he has one of those faces."

"No. I can't put my finger on it. But I'm certain I've seen him before."

Vi tossed down the rag she'd been using to wipe down the table. "You don't want me to be happy, do you?"

I rushed over and wrapped an arm around her. I rested my head on her shoulder. "It's not that. I worry about you." *As much as you fret over me*, I didn't say. "I'm worried that you don't really know who he is and why he would need a place to stay. Doesn't that concern you?"

"What do you think, he's some kind of criminal?"

I would never judge anyone on their appearance.

"I don't know what to think."

"He's good," she spat.

I straightened and held up my hands. "Fine. He seems nice."

Turner had remained quiet, and I was curious about his thoughts but didn't want to put him on the spot. It was obvious he'd held Vi in his confidence. So, I dropped it and helped Vi make a breakfast of biscuits and eggs.

After we were done and the tiny kitchen area cleaned up, Turner said, "Well, I should be going. No doubt they'll be wondering why I haven't appeared for morning chores."

I glanced at his hands, knowing he would use them to fix and build things throughout the day. I thought about how those same hands had held me all night.

"Bye," I said, feeling awkward. I almost thought he would lean over and kiss me, but he didn't.

When the door closed behind him, I turned to face my sister. It was then I let the heat of my anger percolate through my skin. "Is there something you want to tell me about you and Turner?"

"Bailey, I'm sorry."

"How long did you wait after I left town before you pursued him?" I asked.

A righteous indignation crossed over my sister's haunted features. "Why are you back here, Bailey? Why are you getting Turner's hopes up? He deserves better than that."

I paused, surprised to hear her sounding like Father when she'd always been my champion. "Why?" I asked. "So you can have him?"

A horrified look graced her features.

"It wasn't like that. Remember, we're closer in age. I started crushing on him once I realized boys weren't gross."

"You never told me that," I spat, even though I'd known. The hurt I felt flowed through my words.

Her look was now pleading. "You followed him around

like a puppy and wouldn't have understood. You would have told him, thinking it was a joke."

"I didn't follow him around."

She crossed her arms over her chest.

"Okay, but I followed you too. I worshiped you both," I confessed.

"I thought he hung out with you to be around me. Then it turned out, you were the glue to his being around. I don't know when he fell for you. But it was you two that clicked. You were too young, and he never treated you any different than just a friend, so I let it go. Then more and more he came over to hang out with just you."

I sat. No, I flopped down onto the bench in front of the table. My eyes were heavy with guilt. Had I known her feelings for certain, would I have done anything differently? Would Turner have been with my sister and happy if I had backed off? These were questions I would never get answers to. I had part of an answer. If there had been a spark, why didn't he pursue her after I left, and she made herself available?

"What, you're just going to sit there?" she said.

"What do you want me to say?" I hedged.

"Tell me you're not going to break his heart."

I couldn't tell her that. My mouth parted and I confessed my sins.

"There's someone else."

Her eyes widened and I began to tell her the story.

FIFTEEN

PAST

FEELING LIKE MY HEART HAD BEEN BEATEN TO A PULP,
I stood in front of the door a second before I knocked.

Lizzy, as if waiting on the other side until I'd gathered
the last of my courage, flung open the door and hauled me
inside.

"Look at you," she said, pushing strands of dampened
hair from the sides of my face.

"Oh honey." She pulled me into a fierce hug. "He's a
dumb jerk face."

I had to smile. My best friend had far more colorful
words in her vocabulary, but out of consideration for my
time in need said the right things to make me laugh and cry
at the same time.

But what made her my very best friend in the world was
taking me in without notice so close to the holidays.

"Mom's thrilled you'll be spending Christmas with us."
She stepped back as if she understood I didn't want this to
be a thing. "With Matt being a dumb jerk face too, he isn't

coming home. She's looking forward to spoiling someone else besides me."

When I just stood there feeling the chill from the outside temperatures still invading my skin, she snagged my bag from my hand.

"Come, you can have Matty's room. Not like he's coming home anytime soon. It's got its own bath and everything."

She took my hand to get me moving and I followed her into the room. It was spacious, bigger than the bedroom Scott and I had shared. It was painted in shades of gray and blue, but didn't completely look like a bachelor's space.

"Thanks," I managed to say, still hovering in the doorway.

"Stop. I'm so excited to have you here. You know I've always wanted to trade in my brother for a sister."

Her grin was enormous and it was hard to stop my mouth from forming a likewise upward curve.

"Still, I'll pay you rent, and I'll start looking for my own place."

She waved a hand while I couldn't manage to lift my lead feet. "That's nonsense. You just got here. As for rent, forget it. You're my guest for however long you need it."

Her kindness broke the fragile hold I'd had on my emotions. I burst into soul-wrenching sobs. And not so much for the man, but for how stupid I'd been. Gone was the girl who'd run from a society where men ruled. What was in her place was a woman who'd slipped right into the rules of how I'd been raised. I'd trusted a man I shouldn't have because I'd allowed myself to believe that was better than the invisible scarlet S for *sinner* I'd worn for sleeping with a man who wasn't my husband.

She wiped at my tears. "You will not let that scum bucket, limp dick—no, scratch that—tiny dick, no good, lying asshat have this much power over you."

The one thing she hadn't said was *I told you* and I loved her more for that.

"You shower the stink of that jerk face off of you and we are going out for a night on the town."

I shook my head. "I can't. I just want—"

She snapped her finger. "Ice cream."

Slowly, I nodded, wanting to marry her that instant. She was better at sensing my needs than anyone in a long time.

"We'll watch empowering movies like *Kill Bill*, *Thelma and Louise*, or *Carrie*." Her face lit up on the last one. "Or maybe *9 to 5*. Mom made me watch it with her when Turtle Face Timmy called me awful names made me cry."

My smile widened a little more. "You know you're the best."

She nodded. "But don't think we are going to spend every night here. Trust me. We are going out. I'll take you to my favorite little dive bar and—" She got a little more excited. "New Year's Eve, we are going to the best party ever."

True to her word, she'd allowed me to wallow the first night. But after, we'd played pool several nights at her dive bar. Another night we'd wandered into a bar full of Harvard wannabes and didn't last there long. It was so far from Lizzy's scene. We'd eaten at her parents' house a few times, and had dinner at restaurants at others, until that night came.

It was hard to forget that I was supposed to get married that night. I tried and failed as I got ready to go to the big New Year's Eve bash at the fancy hotel Lizzy was taking me to.

"Damn, girl, you look fuckable."

My jaw slackened and I looked at myself in horror.

Lizzy laughed. "Stop. You look great, not like a slut—not exactly." When I made a move to find something else, she giggled. "I'm only kidding. Besides, this night is like Vegas. What happens tonight will disappear when morning comes. We won't speak of it."

I wished I could be as free as she was, but I nodded anyway.

I smoothed a hand down my dress and felt the slight bump from the garters I wore underneath, a gift from my bestie.

"Too bad Matty didn't show up," she said absently.

I turned away, feeling a blush creep up my cheek. Her brother, Matt, was super hot and I'd crushed on him a long time.

She took a final look in the mirror after applying a little more lipstick. "Okay, it's time to crush hearts."

The place was packed, and I felt guarded and nervous. Lizzy went first to the bar and got us two shots each, which we downed before she pulled me onto the dance floor.

It wasn't long before I let the beat dictate my movements. It was several shots later when I completely let loose. My hips as well as the rest of my body had their own mind.

It was one night. What could possibly happen in one night?

Him.

SIXTEEN

"Him?" Violet asked.

I nodded as if that was a good answer. "Like a dream, he just appeared. I couldn't tell you what he said or even how I responded. But I let him lead me off the dance floor in a cataclysmic move that would forever change my life."

Surprise filled her face and I realized I'd said too much.

"You slept with him?"

I shrugged. "Are you going to shame me for it?"

"No," she said adamantly. "It just seems out of character even for you."

It had been. I'd wrestled with it for days after. Thank God for Lizzy.

I continued and told her all about Scott, Kalen, and my job and how it landed me here. I even admitted that I still had lingering feelings for Kalen and that I still loved Turner. I just wasn't sure yet if I was in love with him.

"So this Kalen lied to you?" she asked.

"It wasn't like that," I breathed and admitted what I had time to think about after my initial anger. "He was protecting himself. He's rich and women would want that alone, but he's also extremely handsome. He didn't know me from anyone. In his own way, I think he wanted me to like him and not his money."

She had sat down somewhere along the way of my telling. "If you're in love with this Kalen, you need to let Turner go. He was a wreck after you left. Then he left and went to college too. He came home hopeful every holiday, only you never showed up."

"I did come home once," I said in my defense.

"And look how that turned out." Her face held the expression that said *need I say more?* And no, she didn't. "Margaret still thinks she has a shot. She's not happy about your return."

It looked like many people weren't happy that I was here. It was looking like there wasn't any saneness to my decision to come home as a safe haven.

"You've dodged the question. What happened between you and Turner?" I asked.

She exhaled a breath and avoided an answer. "It's not like the pickings around here are plentiful. They don't grow multiple Turners in this place. Most guys who are easy on the eyes like the backwards lifestyle of *man beats his chest and woman listens.*"

"Did you sleep with him?"

Her mouth opened in shock. "No. We had a moment. He was sad about you and it just happened."

"What happened?"

"We kissed. But it was barely a brush on the mouth before we realized it was wrong. It felt like I was kissing my brother. Honestly, you have nothing to worry about. I love my husband. Turner is just a friend."

There was a pregnant pause before she added, "You have to decide if Turner is just a friend too. He deserves an answer."

I'd been wrong so many times. I wasn't sure if I was capable of making a right decision. I thought it would be easy forgetting Kalen, and I'd been wrong.

SEVENTEEN

SOME SAY YOUR LIFE COMES FULL CIRCLE. SITTING with my two younger sisters while we folded laundry, I thought that might be true.

At twelve and nine, their chatter was still filled with innocence. Rose, in the early stages of preteen, didn't want to talk as much as Poppy. My youngest sister was still just a girl and kept steering the topic of conversation back to Christmas, when she wasn't peppering me with other questions about my life. I didn't mind. She barely knew who I was. She was really young when I left for college.

"Did you have a doll when you were little?" Poppy asked.

"I did." I struggled to remember it. Dolls had been okay in my book, but I had much rather gone out and followed behind Turner. My conversation with Violet reminded me of that.

Out of nowhere, Rose politely said, "Are you going to kiss Turner?" I didn't have time to be shocked before she

103

continued. "Because I heard Father tell Mother that you and Turner should have gotten married."

Okay, there were two problems with her question and subsequent statement. I met Poppy's eyes before she studiously looked away.

The bell tolled from outside, and the girls got to their feet. "School time," Poppy said with glee. She was still at the age where school actually seemed kind of fun.

They gathered their bundle of books, clasped in what looked like straps, and headed out of the house. I wiped down the tables and straightened the chairs and benches. Then there was really nothing to do. I checked the girls' room, but all their clothes were washed, folded, and put away.

In the boys' room, it was a different story. In the interest of something to do, I considered washing their clothes until I came across a pair of boxers. I put everything back the way I found it. Something told me they wouldn't appreciate the intrusion.

What I really wanted was to talk to my mother, but she'd been gone when I arrived. The girls hadn't known just where she was off to. With nothing else to do until afternoon chores, I headed to the schoolhouse to work on reconciling the current bank statement.

It was in the numbers I found some peace. I wasn't sure why, considering it was work that had unraveled my life. I stared at the phone a long time considering. It would be so easy to call Kalen, but I stayed strong.

By lunch, I was hungry and tired. My day had started at the crack of dawn, and I'd been at it almost as long as an average workday when my sister popped her head in.

"I thought you might be hungry," Mary said.

I was able to school my features and not show any surprise. I took the basket of food she held out to me. There were some dried meat and fruits and a bit of cheese. A minute later, she returned with a cup of hot tea.

"Thanks."

She smiled and gave a tiny shrug. "We're sisters."

I felt bad for assuming she had an ulterior motive.

"Are you and Turner together?" she asked.

And there it was. If I'd hoped that she'd truly come for me, I would have been disappointed.

"Who are you asking for? Margaret?"

She shrugged again, this time a bit more exaggerated. "Don't you think she deserves to know?"

"I think it's none of my business," I said slowly, enunciating each word, hoping she'd hear my consternation. "That's between her and him."

"But don't you see? You're the problem. He hasn't let go. He won't truly give her a chance because of you. Just when they were getting close again, you show up."

All pretense of sisterly love was gone. Her distain for me was once again evident.

"I didn't come for him," I said.

Her eyes narrowed and her lips pinched, like she totally didn't believe me. "You could have had him, but you didn't want him. You left and now you're back."

The fact that she said it again annoyed me more because she was right. What was I doing? I tossed my hands up, because what could I say?

"They would have been married if you hadn't come back that Christmas," she tossed out.

"For your wedding," I said. Mary had a way of stretching the truth to suit her purposes. "I didn't make Turner do anything."

"No, you didn't," she said with a sneer. "You just have a way of making the boys lose their heads over you like you're the queen of men or something."

"What is this really about?" I asked because the hate in her tone was off the charts. This was beyond petty jealousies.

"What's going on in here?"

Mary and I turned to find Turner standing in the doorway with his arms crossed over his chest. My sister morphed into something sweet and her quick change bordered on nothing short of psychotic. "Nothing. I brought my sister some tea."

She gestured at the cup before adjusting the sling that was across her body. "Can you hold him while I go outside and check on the kids? He's a heavy sleeper. He shouldn't be a problem. I know you never wanted kids," she said to me.

I ignored her jab and focused on the quiet baby I hadn't noticed before because I'd been focused on my sister's sour face. She placed the bundle in my arms and the baby slept quietly. I cradled the tiny bundle in my arms, feeling a love that only comes from family. It was instant but sure. He was perfect and a little darling.

Turner got on his knees to kneel close to me. With gentle fingers, he brushed the wisp of hair from the baby's forehead.

"What's this about you not wanting kids?"

I'd hoped that he'd overlooked the dig my sister got in. I'd said that once when we were younger.

"It was just something I said in anger one of those times when we had to babysit instead of hanging out with everyone else." I didn't say that everyone else really just meant him.

"Oh," he said, looking up at me. "Do you want to have kids?"

Mary's hope had been for Turner to see we weren't compatible. And now I wondered if she was right. I hadn't thought much about making a family. It was something that had been so expected of me, once I was free of this place, I hadn't given that much thought.

Would I want to bring up my kids the same way I'd been? Did I even want the responsibility of it?

I raised my arms to lift my nephew so I could place a gentle kiss on his forehead. It was probably the last time I'd get to hold him the way Mary was acting. I didn't want to be around her. As I lowered him, he cooed. It wasn't that loud, but a mother's instinct was apparently powerful.

Mary came back in a rush. With the door to the office open, I saw her return. "He's probably hungry."

Then she proceeded to unbutton her shirt. Turner looked away. Likely not comfortable with seeing my sister's naked breast. As a kid, it was just a way of life. As an adult, she was my sister baring her breast to the world, too weird for me.

"We should go and give you privacy," I stated, getting to my feet.

Turner did the same with his gaze anywhere but at her. My guess was that Mary wouldn't have minded one bit if

Turner saw her. I headed out the door and drew in a heavy breath once outside.

The kids were sitting picnic style on the small front lawn eating lunch and talking. Turner took my hand. "Want to go for a walk?"

The need for air and distance from Mary filled me. I nodded.

EIGHTEEN

KALEN

THE NEWS WASN'T GOOD.

"What are you going to do?" Griffin asked.

I'd never left my son for more than a day since he was born. But what we'd learned in the last few hours chilled my bones. Someone was after Bailey.

Griffin had gotten a lead on her after placing a call to the car rental company she'd used. He flirted with the woman and talked her into giving up some information. She'd even laughed and admitted that someone else had called asking similar questions.

"I have to go," I said.

I thought about the meetings I would miss, but none of that mattered. I was certain she was in danger because of me. The community she'd grown up in wasn't equipped to handle the possible threat headed their way, according to Griffin.

"Do you want me to go with you?" he asked.

I shook my head. "I need you to stay here and protect my son."

Because someone wanted to destroy me, and I wasn't sure to what lengths they were willing to go.

"Or you could stay here with yer wee bairn, and I could go? You've already said the lass is cross with yer."

"No," I said definitively.

For that point I was firm. The need to protect her was primal, something I didn't quite understand. What I did know was that I wouldn't be able to think clearly until I knew she was safe with my own eyes.

"I should be back in a day," I said.

Once I found her, she would see reason and come back with me where I could make sure she was protected.

"How are you getting there?"

With single-minded focus, I began to plan. How my father would feel about me rearranging my schedule was the least of my worries.

NINETEEN

Walking down the center aisle of the road wasn't a problem, considering cars weren't allowed in the community unless there was an emergency. Something that never happened in the years I'd lived here.

We hadn't gone far before he ducked us into the tree line.

"I heard you and Vi this morning," I said.

Turner stopped in his tracks and faced me. "What happened between her and me was a mistake."

"And what happened exactly?" Although I may not have been privy to most of the details of his life after me, somehow, I felt like I deserved this bit of truth, seeing that she was my sister.

"You have to understand, losing you was like losing my life. She was there. And in a moment of weakness, I gave in. She'd been so close. I can't even remember how it happened. But I got lost in her eyes, and it was as if you were there. And I kissed her. But as soon as it happened, I knew it wasn't you."

"Does she know that?"

He shook his head. "She knows that I couldn't do it. But I never told her it was you I was seeing. I didn't think that was the right thing to say. Kissing her had been shitty enough."

Curious, I asked, "And Margaret?" Although we'd talked about it before, I thought there may have been more to that story.

He stepped closer; his eyes darkened with desire. "Margaret made her idea of us together known. She was persistent. I'd broken up with my girlfriend at school and was back at home. I wasn't in the mood for any girl. Then you showed up. She was convenient. And I used her. I felt like a total douche after. But I wanted you to hurt as much as I did."

I closed my eyes and leaned back on a nearby tree. Now his guilt was mine, as inadvertently I'd caused Margaret's pain as well.

Since we were getting everything out in the open, I asked, "You had a girlfriend?"

"Carrie," he said frankly. "She was from a small town and we had a lot in common."

"Pretty?" That was a dumb question. Turner was as hot as they came.

He lifted his shoulders quickly in a dismissive gesture. "Sure."

"Why'd you break up?" Now I was crossing the line into none of my business territory. If he didn't answer, I wouldn't press him. It wasn't like I wanted to talk about Kalen or Scott.

"She wasn't you."

Looking up into his lovely eyes, I saw the pain again. "I should hope not," I teased. "If I had a twin that my parents didn't tell me about, I'd be pretty pissed."

He laughed, and my joke to ease the tension worked. Turner, however, wasn't done with his confession. "In the end we wanted different things. She wanted the house and all the trappings. Small-town life had made her dream of grander things."

"Nothing wrong with that," I said, playing devil's advocate.

"It wasn't that. She was into the things." He punctuated that last word.

I lifted my head in acknowledgment. "She was materialistic."

"Exactly. She just didn't want a bigger house. She wanted the biggest house on the block so she could flaunt her success to everyone she left behind."

That was one way of losing him, I thought to myself. "She didn't know you very well."

"I didn't know her either until it was too late."

It was on the tip of my tongue to ask what he was doing with her that kept him from asking the important questions, but I decided it wasn't an answer I wanted to know.

"That's the thing I love most about you, Bailey. You *get* me like no one else."

Trying to stop this from where it was headed as he moved closer to me, I blurted, "What if I wanted the biggest house and car?"

"I'd give you those things and fill it with our kids."

My lips felt dry. I licked them as he slowly stalked the

small distance between us. "You're not worried about my wanting things?"

He chuckled. "You care less about things than I do. Give the girl plumbing and electricity here, and you might stay."

"Maybe." And that was the last word before the heat between us ignited like a bomb.

His eyes explored my body like he had X-ray vision. His desire became tangible and sparked my own. When his hand tangled in my hair, he stared at my mouth like I could quench his thirst. My lips tingled as anticipation lit a charge inside me.

"This dress should be labeled cockblocker," he hissed.

I looked at the fabric that covered me completely. His hands disengaged and reached my hips, fisting the fabric. Slowly, he pulled it higher to reveal my calves and then my knees.

He descended to kneel before me so fast I had no time to stop him. Then reverently he looked up at me with the hem of my dress held at thigh level. There in his eyes, I saw the answer he sought.

There was nothing to stop me but my conscience because I belonged to no one but myself.

We were adults, and it wasn't as if this was our first time. We'd seen each other's skin.

Yet, Kalen's face replaced Turner's for a second and a guilt I shouldn't feel filled me.

As if a higher power sensed my indecision, the school bell tolled as a reminder not only to the students but to the entire community that break was over.

Turner stood and adjusted himself. With a quick raise of the eyebrows, he said, "They'll be looking for me."

My mouth felt dry and as swollen as my guilt. He'd been passionate when we were young. But this Turner acted like a man very much in control of how to pleasure a woman. The thought of how many women had helped him learn his tricks of the trade made me queasy.

"I'll head back," he said.

Now I *did* frown. "You don't want me to walk with you?"

He shook his head. "I want you to walk with me, ride me, marry me, and bear my children. But if you come with me now, I'm afraid everyone will know just how much I want my child growing inside you."

His sexy grin made my heart flutter. I watched him walk away until I couldn't see him anymore. Then I sat and rested my head against the cold tree. What the hell had I almost done? How had things spun out of control so fast? This was going to complicate things. I loved him. I did.

I just couldn't stop thinking of Kalen. I hated him and wanted him all the same.

Lizzy made me question my decision. If only I could get a sign. Something that would give me the answers to the questions in my heart.

TWENTY

KALEN

Jolted awake, I stared into moonlit eyes. They sparkled with wicked intention.

"Lass, you're back."

She nodded and crawled between my legs, pulling the fabric of the sheets down from my body. She had an agenda and my dick jumped on board. Her tongue flicked from her mouth and slowly wet her parted lips.

All the blood left my extremities, heading to where all my goals would be met. My mind wavered, wondering how she'd gotten in. When the sheet cleared my cock for takeoff, I didn't care how she got in. I was just glad she was here.

A bead of pre-cum dotted my dick, letting her know just what spot needed her immediate attention. Bailey was always good at following directions, even unsaid ones. Her pink tongue snaked out of her mouth and licked after the trail until she captured the drop.

As shadowy as my room was, her eyes were bright and wide on me. The combination of her stare and her mouth on me caused a few more drops to form at the summit of my erection.

She gave me a grin, reminding me how good she was at blowjobs and keeping the grazing of teeth to a minimum. Only ever enough to cause pleasure and not pain. With hollowed cheeks, she used suction on the crown of my arousal like a champ. She deserved a fucking prize. Whatever she wanted, she just had to ask.

"Fuck, lass. I need to be inside you."

Her head nodded slightly, sending the dark blaze of her hair cascading around her shoulders. I reached out with a hand to tug her to me, needing to taste her mouth. Having her here meant nights without her would forever be at an end. I wouldn't let her go this time. Screw the lawyers; they'd have to figure out a way around it.

When she maneuvered to a kneeling position, I finally got a view of her beautiful breasts. They swayed with nipples pebbled, awaiting my hungry mouth. There was no way I wasn't getting a handful. When I reached out, she leaned back again, shaking her head silently.

"Why, lass? Why won't you let me touch you?"

No answer, only another shake of her head. When she raised up to position my cock at her entrance, I forgot it all. Need consumed all thoughts. It was more important than anything else. If she wanted to control this encounter, I'd let her.

The glide down my length was a tight-fisted pressure. I wanted to grip her hips and control the pace. But again, she wouldn't let me touch her, which was its own sweet torture. The idea of being tied up started to give new meaning in my mind. Next time, she would be the one forced to feel and not touch.

Her hips rose and fell in a rhythm that meant I wouldn't last. "Lass, you're going to have to slow down if you don't want me to come." It had been too long with me not inside her for me to hold on much longer.

She leaned forward, causing her breasts to tempt me, right in front of my face yet just out of reach. Her hips continued to twist and ride me with precision. "Are you ready, lass?"

Her head dropped, and her hair fanned in front of her, causing a curtain to hide her face. After swiveling her hips a few more times, she threw back her head and stared me in the face. My hands fisted the sheet, trying hard to respect her desire for me not to touch her.

When her sheath fisted around me and her head nodded, I was past the point of no return. "Come with me," I pleaded with readiness as my balls tightened in the final stages of release.

I jerked awake when hot streams jetted onto my chest. My breathing labored while my hand continued to pump my release as the dream of Bailey faded far too quickly for my liking.

My emotions roiled. I wasn't sure if I was satisfied or pissed off. I hadn't had a wet dream since my early teens. I hopped out of bed and strode to my bathroom, needing a shower. I'd never allowed a woman to hold me prisoner by the balls the way Bailey did. This would end tonight, one way or another.

TWENTY-ONE

After walking back to the schoolhouse, reconciling the community's books turned out to be a great distraction. Everything was in order as expected. By nightfall, I headed to Violet's.

When I entered, Turner and Steven were sitting at the table as Vi worked on dinner. My eyes locked with Turner's and my stomach did funny things.

It wasn't as though I'd forgotten Kalen. I just remembered Turner and all his sugar and spice that made everything nice for me growing up.

He stood, stepping over the bench to stand before me.

"I want to finish what we started before," he whispered into my ear, causing me to blush.

The redness that filled my cheeks wasn't the only part of my body that betrayed me. My body tightened at the promise of what could be.

He took my hand, leading me back to the table as my heart, brain, and core warred over two men. One wanted me with the desperation that I read in his eyes when we parted ways. The other loved me like no other man had before.

In a fantasy world, I could have them both. But the truth was, I'd given one up. I'd vowed to set him free with no turning back. Yet, part of me still hadn't let go, not completely.

Turner continued being a presence I couldn't deny as he placed his hand on the middle of my back after we sat and rubbed soothing circles as if he knew the comfort I sought.

"How was everyone's day?" I asked.

Turner quickly responded, "Busy."

Before Violet's husband, whom I still couldn't read, could speak, my sister walked over.

"Dinner's served," Violet cut in, setting a spit roasted bird on the table. She turned to grab a plate of corn on the cob and place settings for us before I could get up to offer to help.

"Thanks, sis," I said.

Her grin filled the room with such warmth, I felt more at ease with her choice of husband. Still, there was something about him I couldn't quite put my finger on. It felt as though there were secrets in this house not yet exposed.

"What I would do for a beer," Steven said.

I looked toward the floor cubby that held beer the night before.

Violet answered her husband before I could think of a response. "You could make a beer run," she said and glanced my way.

Steven followed her gaze, his chin steepled on the top of

his fingertips with his elbows perched on top of the table. Then he sat up straight and the gleam in his eyes said *trouble* as he turned to me. "How did you get here?"

My mouth opened, but I knew what my answer meant.

He pointed at me. "You have a car."

There was no point in lying. "It's parked all the way at the front of the compound." It was an attempt to make it sound like an avenue not worth pursuing.

"Let's go," he said, like it was a forgone conclusion. "We'll get beer and maybe some cards. We could play poker."

Automatically, I looked at Violet. Everything he spoke of was against the rules. If Father found out, we would be done for. It could jeopardize my being in the community. But there on my sister's face was a huge grin.

I looked at Turner. His mouth turned up to that telltale sign that said *why not?*

And so, that's how we ended up slinking in the shadows and heading for the front gate. The fact that we had to hide our exploits should have been good enough reason for us not doing this. We might be stopped and queried about where we were going. Leaving the compound for business not approved by the council was frowned upon. Whatever we did on the outside would be scrutinized by the public.

Just when the security building came into sight, there was a squeal behind me. I turned to see Steven had swept my sister off her feet and gazed at her like she was the light of his life. In that moment, I saw the man my sister had fallen for.

Turner used that opportunity to hug me around the

waist and pull me close. Heat flared between us, and I could envision his lips on mine as fire passed between us.

"I feel like a teenager again," Violet said from behind us. "Like we are sneaking away from the house to go make out."

She spoke like there had been lots of moments to do such things when we grew up when there had not. Though I understood. Being with Turner like this did remind me of a past I'd walked away from.

"I should probably go in alone," I said. "Father is going to find out that I left. He'll discover sooner if you guys are with me."

Everyone nodded in agreement. Violet giggled like the thought of getting into trouble might just be worth all the hassle.

I brushed my fingers along the brick façade before I turned the corner to the front of the building. My car was still the lone one in the tiny lot of four slots.

After I retrieved my keys, I made an executive decision and got clothes from my trunk. In the visitors' building bathroom, I changed. Doug was on duty today and didn't say much. When I stepped out wearing form-fitting jeans and a deep V top, Doug gave me an ardent smile. I skipped out the door, not wanting him to make a comment.

When I met up with the others, Turner gave me a lingering look over. He hadn't ever seen me in anything outside of the shapeless floor-length dresses we wore.

"I think only one of us goes in to buy anything." I looked over at Turner for his approval. He nodded but had a funny expression that I couldn't read on his face. Alone, I pulled the car back and into the shadows, away from the front of the building and its windows.

Once I stopped, my cohorts got in. Doug had already opened the gate, and I made for it without hesitation. If he was watching the camera, he would see the four heads in the car because of the security lamps that pointed outwards from the building. However, I hoped he wasn't paying that much attention.

I made a left at the dead end private road to head out to the main one.

By the time we made it to the gas station that had a mini mart attached, I practically jumped out of the car.

Turner opened the door, but I shooed him to stay in. His clothing was too conspicuous.

Steven gave me his drink request from the back seat. It wasn't hard to forget Bud Light. He also requested Jack Daniels, but I didn't think this place sold liquor.

The bell chimed at my entrance, and I zoned in on the back wall with the clear refrigerator doors that held drinks of all kinds, including soda and water. I scanned them as I walked by until I found the one filled with cases of beer. I grabbed a twelve pack.

Two doors down, I found something for Violet and me to drink. The selection wasn't full of choices, so I picked two bottles of decent-looking wine and walked up to the counter, where the TV was showing a program.

The narrator droned on, "*As you can tell from that last picture, it's not surprising King is the talk of the celebrity gossip. With headlines of possible embezzlement, we all wonder what Kinsey St. Clair, socialite and billion-dollar heiress to her father's dynasty, was doing on King's arm. Is it merger talks, a takeover, or maybe just two beautiful people*

*out for a night on the town? Stay with us, folks. We will keep
you posted with the latest."*

The logo of a popular gossip TV and magazine
company popped up just before a commercial. They hadn't
shown any other pictures. But from the glimpse I'd caught, I
knew that man... He'd already moved on and I had no one
to blame but myself.

"Miss," the clerk inquired.

I followed his finger to the total on the register. I
reached into my wallet and pulled out a credit card before
stopping myself. For some reason, I thought about how I
could be tracked by purchases. I didn't think I was in any
danger. Still, I handed the clerk cash and waited for my
change.

My mind fogged on the ride home as I thought about
what I'd seen. The pain in my chest at seeing Kalen with
another woman on his arm gripped my heart in a tight fist.
How wrong I'd been about him. Some part of me had hung
on, hoping that maybe...

My head was still messed up when I parked back in the
visitors' lot in the community. I was unaware of the conversation all around me as the sense of loss consumed me. I
hadn't felt this bad when Scott had cheated on me. I'd felt
foolish then. This was different. I was still standing, half-
dressed, in the bathroom when Turner came in. So much
for Doug not knowing that I'd taken others with me.

"What's wrong? You've barely spoken a word since you
walked into the gas station. Did you see something? Did
something happen about the case? I saw the TV in there."

"No," I whispered. Standing in my bra and jeans, I felt
dazed. "I'll be fine."

When he drew me close and enveloped me in his arms, I felt something open inside me that I'd longed for since I first left home all those years ago.

In his eyes, I let myself accept what he was offering. He bent and pressed his lips to mine, and I melted into him. I grabbed on to something real, and I kissed him back. I tugged at his neck and reached for his pants.

"Whoa," he said, stilling my wrist. "Not in here. Doug will figure out what we are up to, and it will be all over town before morning."

He was right, so I stepped back and finished getting dressed while Turner watched. After putting my change of clothes into my trunk, I went back in to give my car keys back to Doug. I realized then what a waste of money the rental car was. I should return it and call for a cab when I was ready to leave, if ever.

Turner gently tugged on my hand while I stood there in thought. I didn't have to decide tonight. I would worry about that in the morning when I figured out what my short-term plans were.

"Where are Vi and Steven?" I asked.

Turner, still guiding me down the road, answered, "They went ahead."

He wasn't carrying the bags, so I assumed they had them.

"We don't have to stay long," Turner said. "We'll have a few drinks and play some cards, and then I'll take you back to my place."

I nodded, knowing what would happen there. And why not? Kalen had moved on. Turner was here.

We made it back to Violet's house, and soon my despair

was gone along with one of the two bottles of wine. Steven turned out to be kind of funny.

Violet was doing a happy dance after winning the last hand. "Drink up, guys," she announced after she finished her twirl with hands waving in the air.

In place of liquor, we were doing shots of beer or wine according to a game Steven taught us. The wine was really sweet, and I found I didn't mind drinking it at all. The second bottle of wine was half-empty. Violet was so cute drunk. She probably hadn't been drunk a day in her life.

"Let's play truth or dare," Violet said.

There was something enticing about the idea.

"Okay. Your turn," I pronounced as I stared at her mysterious husband.

"Ask away," Steven dared.

I took it to mean he'd chosen truth. Fine by me.

"Why are you here?"

He held my gaze as he answered, "Probably for the same reasons you are."

I almost blurted *I was running away*, but caught myself. Though it was true, it wasn't how I wanted things for Turner and me to start.

"My turn," Steven said as I stared at him.

He'd answered before like he was certain of my answer. What was he running from?

"Turner," Steven said, "have you told Bailey of your plans?"

My head snapped in Turner's direction. The fact that Steven hadn't given Turner the option of truth or dare was forgotten. Now I just wanted to know the answer to the question Steven posed, reminding me of his conversation with Violet that morning.

"Plans?"

Turner moved faster than my sluggish brain could make out. Arms snaked around my waist as he whispered into my ear, "I'll tell you later."

"I like where his head's at," Steven said. "Come on, wife. I need that pretty mouth of yours."

Footsteps receded as Turner scooped me up. Automatically, I wrapped my legs around his waist and let him carry me off.

"I need you," he said and I nodded.

As he walked the few feet to the tiny bedroom on the opposite side of the house that I'd been using, two pairs of eyes filled my head. Kalen and Margaret.

My vision, which had been muddled, cleared up a bit. I leaned back to stare into Turner's big brown eyes and asked the question that knotted my belly. "Have you slept with Margaret?"

Though I had no right to ask, his answer mattered. In that moment, I very much knew how she'd feel if she knew what was about to happen.

"Now is not the time," he said, untangling my legs and setting me on my feet.

"Was she better than me?" I asked, looking up, wanting not to read into his non-answer. My voice sounded like a small child in need of approval. It was like having an out-of-body experience. I could see the train wreck coming, but I couldn't stop it.

Turner pulled me close. "No one's better than you," he said softly.

The door was still open. I could tell him to go and sleep off the hurricane of emotions I felt.

Instead, my mouth spoke without direction from my brain. "Be honest. Does she have a claim on you?"

Because the words had spilled out of me, they were of the old ways. I needed to know if Turner had officially courted Margaret like Mary said or was that what Margaret wanted.

"Only one woman has ever held claim over me, and that is you."

Actions spoke louder than any words. So I closed the door and walked over to the bed in invitation.

Some part of me knew this act would break the final bond I felt toward Kalen. And maybe that was a little unfair. But Turner had to be the one, didn't he? He'd never let me down, not once. I would be stupid not to see the light when it was such a beacon in front of me.

When he moved toward me, I tried not to let any part of me remember Kalen's touch as Turner worked the buttons on my dress. If he only knew how many levels he was freeing me by just being him.

As my dress fell, he sank once again to his knees and waited. This time there was no hesitation on my part. I nodded, giving him the approval he sought.

Then with my dress but a puddle around me, his hands warmed my thighs as they skimmed up them, reaching my covered center. He didn't waste time with the removal of that garment as he trailed kisses in the wake of his hands from my thighs until his tongue danced toward the seam of my underwear. I felt the shift of the scrap of fabric to the side a second before my stomach lurched.

I stumbled out of his hold with enough time to step into my dress and pull it up enough to cover the important bits.

Turner's eyes popped wide, and I reached for the door. My stomach must have made a sound, or it was my hand that covered my mouth while the rest of me turned a sickly green that clued him in. He stepped forward, and I yanked the door open. I don't think I could have moved that fast if the idea of cleaning my sister's floor hadn't pushed my loopy legs out the back door.

The projectile of my vomit didn't clear the stairs. I was still retching when Turner's palm rubbed at my back. I eliminated everything in my body, including my stomach. Surely it came up with the rest. I coughed and gagged some more before everything finally subsided.

"Are you okay?" he asked.

I managed a nod as he spoke on.

"For a second, I thought maybe it was me and you just didn't want to, you know."

He laughed and I found myself with a half-grin, half-sour look. "Sorry."

He held my face in his tender hands and kissed my forehead. "I'll go get the bucket." He handed me a towel from out of nowhere. "I would kiss you, but you still have a bit there in the corner of your mouth."

Mortified, even though he wore a smile, I swiped at my face and looked at my hand in the moonlight. The smell of whatever it was hit my nose, and I began dry heaving.

When he came back, the bucket was full. Apparently, the pipes weren't frozen. He took the towel still in my hand and dipped a clean corner in before handing the rag back to me. I wiped at my mouth while he doused the stairs with water and went for more. I stood a distance away, wanting to help but afraid my stomach would roll in anger.

When the stairs were free from all that I'd puked, we headed back inside. He closed the door and stepped to me, taking his time to undress me. This was the moment I longed for indoor plumbing.

Turner stood gazing at me, waiting on my cues to tell him what I needed. The way he took care of me melted every part of me.

In the tiny room, I just stood there and watched his expression in the moonlight coming through the small window. My clothes hit the floor and I was left in my bra and panties.

His hand grasped a corner of the quilt and lifted it. I got inside and waited. He, however, fell across the other small bed not three feet away in the tiny room.

"You're not going to lie with me?"

"As much as I want to, I can't be good right now. And you need to sleep. We have tomorrow."

Unable to protest and suddenly very tired, I closed my eyes and soon fell asleep.

I woke to words I longed to hear. "Lass, there you are. I'm sorry it took me so long to get here."

"Kalen."

His hands touched my bare skin, and I wondered when I had completely undressed.

"It's been too long, lass. I can't wait any longer to be inside you."

He was between my legs. He raised my hips, and I felt the tip of him nudge at my opening. "God, I love..."

I waited. I waited for him to say *you* at the end of that sentence.

"To be inside you." With one thrust he filled me. He hadn't prepared me and it had been so long. There was a flash of pain before I rode the currents of pleasure from his movements. He rocked into me over and over again. His cry of orgasm sent me tumbling into bliss.

TWENTY-TWO

Dawn was like the splash of warm water that brought me from the murky depths of sleep. Turner slept like he was on a dock with one leg hanging off the side of a bed that was too small for his tall frame and myself to share.

Kalen wasn't there. Yet, my dreams of him had been vivid. I got up and decided it was best to go to my parents' to freshen up. Though, my dreams had been silent and my own, Turner had still been there. Thankfully sleeping, not aware of how my subconscious thoughts were cheating on us.

Being at home allowed the shame of my behavior last night, and my dreams, to fill my heart. Though I'd come so far in owning my choices, being here I felt that empowerment slipping through my fingers.

I walked in and found my mother at the table folding laundry.

"Mother." It had only been two days, but it felt like a lifetime.

She opened her arms, and I skirted the table to fly into

them. She smelled like home, and I had missed her more over the last few years than I realized.

When my body shook with tears streaming down my face, she stroked my hair and asked, "What's wrong?"

After my sobs subsided, I told her in hushed tones, "I just missed you."

The dim morning light wasn't enough yet to wake my siblings, but I knew they would be up soon.

"This doesn't have anything to do with Kalen or Turner, does it?" she said, framing my face with her hands.

I'd been so determined to walk away from Kalen forever, yet seeing him on the TV with another woman on his arm had shaken me. So much so, I dived too quickly into starting something with Turner. I told her as much.

She looked at me without judgment. "He loves you, you know?"

I nodded.

"I can't blame him. You're beautiful inside and out," she continued, "but as hard as this is, you need to make a choice."

I didn't feel very beautiful. I made a mess of everything I touched. Leaving Scott should have made my world better. Instead, I'd been making all the wrong decisions since.

"Kalen's already made his choice," I complained.

"You did tell him to move on."

I had, but I hadn't expected him to do it the very next day. "I know."

"And you can't choose Turner by default. That wouldn't be fair to him either."

"I know," I repeated.

"Trust your heart. More importantly, trust yourself. I think deep down you know what you want to do. And it's okay if you choose neither." She held my gaze until I gave her a plaintive smile. "Go wash up before your brothers hog all the water," she said. "Don't worry. I won't tell your father."

With a confidence I didn't quite feel, I stood relieved at unloading my burden. Lizzy had always been good for that. I missed her too and would call her later.

After brushing my teeth and hair and a general full-body cleaning, I stepped back into the kitchen and helped my mother finish breakfast as the rest of my siblings fought over the leftover tepid water.

My father stepped into the house as we started to put breakfast on the table. I wasn't surprised he hadn't been home. I was certain my mother wouldn't have encouraged a chat if he had been.

He barely glanced my way. I tried not to be hurt by it. I didn't see him as a bad man no matter how he saw me. I was a practical one. Everything was black and white. There wasn't any such thing as the murky gray that colored my life.

Once we were all seated around the table, my father commanded, "Bailey, grace the food."

Jake snickered and I shot him a glare. Scott hadn't been religious and college life, well, we just didn't say prayers before meals, not out loud at least.

Rusty, I stumbled through it as my siblings snickered, until I was done. Father's scowl quieted everyone. After amen was said, the noise ratcheted up as the younger ones fought to get to the food first after Father got his.

As we ate, Father dictated our duties for the day. I gave silent points to my siblings for not outwardly groaning. No one dared to utter a sound of protest. When the meal was over, I asked to speak to both of my parents. Not wanting to let my younger siblings hear what I had to say, I urged my parents outside.

I didn't stop at the porch. I kept going a few more feet, trying to put as much distance between us and the house as possible.

On the way out, Father put his hat on, and I stared at his neatly trimmed beard. It was long but well kempt. He wasn't a great deal taller than me, but it felt like he towered over me as he did when I was a child. Though I respected him, I couldn't hold my tongue on this issue.

"What do you know about Vi's husband Steven?" There, I'd said it. Although he seemed nice, I got this feeling he was hiding something big. I couldn't get past Vi's admission she married him because he needed a place to live.

Father stared at me as his hand came up to stroke his beard.

The fact that Mother said nothing as she waited for my father to speak only emphasized why I could never live here. Women were expected to submit to their husbands in all things. And I was a bit too outspoken for that. And even though Turner would have never held me to that standard, he would have been the laughingstock of all the men in the community if he couldn't keep me in line.

"You think that I did not look into the man that married your sister?" he asked. I looked up, ready to answer when his eyes silenced me. "Though he came back clean, I warned Violet not to get involved with a man so new to our community. She begged me to allow her to be with him. She's made her bed." His last phrase sounded exactly like what Mary said. I shouldn't have been surprised. Mary was a *brown-noser*.

"And that's it?" I blurted. My tone raised, and my mother gave me a look of rebuke.

"Bailey, I know it's been a while since you've lived at home, but as you well know, I allow my children to make their choices. Those choices you have to live with."

His eyes bore into mine. He didn't say she had to live with it, but I had to. It all came back to me.

"We police our own. If your sister came to me and told me she felt threatened in any way, I would be there for her. She hasn't. You need to let it go too."

It wasn't so much as I thought he was hurting her as much as I thought he might be hiding from the world. *Like me*, I thought. But what was he hiding from, and would it put my sister in danger? Again, I thought about my own situation. I should leave. I didn't want to believe that someone was after me, but the hairs on my arm rose as I thought about all the warnings that had been sent my way.

My brothers came out. "Bailey said she would chaperone us," Jake said to Father.

That put the spotlight squarely on me as I saw my father's disapproval.

"I will, and I will leave for New York the next day," I said.

Was that a hint of a smile I saw on my father's lips?

"Stop dawdling. Go to your post," Father dictated before walking away.

Mother smiled at me and went inside to herd the rest of

my siblings out for the day. Not wanting to put her between my father and me, I let the matter go.

I spent the rest of the morning chores with my mother and my younger sisters in the kitchen, keeping my thoughts to myself.

My brothers had headed to the stables where they helped with the horses. Anyone from the outside seeing how my family disbursed might assume we lived in a sexist society. While on the surface that was somewhat true, we all learned how to do basic tasks, including cooking, sewing, how to care for animals, plant crops, and other tasks. We were all prepared to be self-sufficient in case we were faced with survival on our own.

When it became apparent an individual had talent in a particular area, they were sent to apprentice with someone skilled in that area. My sisters were still young enough that they were underfoot of my mother. But my brothers had shown a desire to work with horses and other animals we raised here.

Father was a crop farmer. Yet, he let them go work with Isaac in the stables. I was sure Father hoped that one of us would take over the family business so to speak.

As for me, I showed a desire for working with numbers and money. I had often wanted to handle the transactions at market. So I'd been sent to work with Betty on the book-keeping.

Today, I spent time doing manual labor, and by the end of the day, I was so tired, I ate dinner with my family. I ended up crashing with my little sisters, too tired to make the trek to Violet's house. Guiltily, I used my father's reasoning of needing to leave things alone as an excuse. Vi had made it two years with her husband, and she was still alive. I had to trust she'd keep one more night without my help.

When morning came the next day, I felt rested, having had a dreamless night. My sisters were bustling about. I got to my feet to help with breakfast. When the younger ones headed off to school, I followed.

It was time to get lost in the numbers again. Plus, I'd gotten the key from my father so I could use a computer to check my email.

That was my first stop and I only had one message.

It's important that I speak with you, lass.

I let the mouse pointer hover over the delete button. Then I clicked reply.

~~There's nothing that important~~

I started again.

There is nothing left to say. Please stop contacting me.

I shut down the computer and locked the room on my way out. I made the short walk to the schoolhouse and lost myself in the numbers. I made new schedules and a profit and loss statement based on what I learned in school. It was a different format than what they were used to, but I hoped it would be beneficial to those who made decisions based on the profitability of our community businesses.

When Mary brought me lunch, I barely looked up. The cynical part of me guessed she'd been directed to bring me food. When she didn't say a word, I was certain I was right.

Though I could have, I didn't speak to her either. I didn't want to fight about the imaginary things in her head. We were sisters, and she had no reason to hate me. But she did.

Turner hadn't come by, nor did he come to Violet's house that night. And I found myself disappointed.

My eyes closed that night, not sure what tomorrow would bring.

Fingers stroked my core, making me moan as soft lips nibbled insistently at my pulse point. For a second, I thought he might bite me as his teeth grazed my neck.

Desire for him raged like a wildfire and I didn't care if he drew blood. I needed him like I needed to draw breath. I ached so much as I watched him take a step back.

Slowly, like he enjoyed me watching him, he unbuttoned his shirt. It parted, revealing a muscled chest that belonged in magazines. When it hit the floor, I was practically drooling for the main event.

He flicked open the top of his pants and they hung on the edge of his hips. A deep V of corded muscles aimed at my most wanted desire. I was on the verge of begging him to fill me with that hard cock of his, drawing pleasure on the knife's edge of pain. How could one man give me such intense feelings that sent me into bliss every time?

"Kalen," I cried out.

My eyes flew open as thunder cracked the air. I swallowed down the memory of the man I could never have as the sound of water pellets beat against the window like it wanted inside.

One might think that with rain it would be like a day off. But it wasn't. Many chores still needed doing regardless of the weather, and others were just moved indoors.

My arms ached from the work I'd done the day before yesterday, so I opted to review the ledgers. I wondered how the community leaders would feel if I suggested doing the books on a computer instead of paper. It wasn't like they were completely against technology.

Turner blew in the door at lunch. He closed us in the tiny office while noise from conversations in the classroom hid everything we said.

He planted himself at the edge of my desk. Arms folded, he stared at me for a long moment. I kept quiet, waiting for him to speak. He called my bluff and held out for me to break first. No doubt he'd figured out that I was avoiding him. But I wasn't going to capitulate. I grabbed a roll from the basket he brought and bit off a chunk.

Though he tried not to, his quick smile turned to a laugh as he shook his head. His arms uncrossed, and he gently brushed strands of hair from my face. His lips were far too close and the warmth of him filled all the spaces around me.

"You know you can be honest with me," he said.

It wasn't something he needed to say, yet it was something I needed to hear. I let loose the breath that I'd been holding. "I'm afraid."

Pinched or not, his smile was still friendly as he sat back. "Him?" The one-word question showed just how close we still were despite the time that put a wedge between us.

"I don't want to hurt anyone, let alone you. What if—"

"Yeah, what if. What if the sky turned green? What if the moon turned red?" His words got softer as his head dipped. "What if we never found out if this was meant to be?"

There was no doubt about our feelings for each other. My only question was my feelings for Kalen. As much as I wanted to discount them because he'd moved on, better yet, I let him go. Like my mother said, it wouldn't be fair to Turner if I was with him and carried a torch for another.

"Just give us a chance, Bails. Let's go to the dance. No pressure."

I looked up at him, thinking about how close we'd come to crossing a line that wasn't casual the way we'd been raised. A roll in the hay between consenting adults was one thing. Sex with a former lover and friend was a totally different thing. It could never be merely casual.

His direct line into reading my emotions was still active because he said, "We don't have to have sex." He paused and stood up. "Don't get me wrong. Every moment I'm around you, I want you. But I can wait."

There, he'd done it. He'd said what I'd been unable to. It seemed like it was harder now to be so open with him. My guilt for leaving him so long ago made me question if he could ever trust me.

"Look," he said. "I have a lot of things I need to do before I finish for the day. I'll pick you up at Vi's at sunset."

He didn't give me time to answer or to explain that I'd

told my father I would leave. He pressed his lips to mine and strolled out the door. The sounds from the other room filled the brief silence before the door closed again. I peeked into the basket he'd brought and smiled. Talk about non-traditional roles. Wasn't I the one supposed to bring him lunch?

Needing Lizzy, I picked up the phone and dialed her number.

"Hello," she said cautiously.

"Lizzy," I said. My glee might have been a bit too loud. The room next door seemed to quiet just a bit.

"Bails," she called out over the phone. "God, I miss you."

"Me too," I said a lot softer.

"Bails," she said again and the timbre in her voice was full of apology. I understood immediately what she was going to say next. "I'm not sure if you—"

"I saw," I cut her off, not wanting Kalen to take up the little time we had to talk. "What about you? How is Chicago?"

"It's great." But it was Lizzy who was great. She wouldn't press me. "You know, Matt wants you to come for a visit."

"I just bet he does." I laughed.

"Ewww, that's seriously gross, the two of you." She paused. "He's a great guy, though."

"I know. I think I've had my fill of guys." I told her everything that had happened in excruciating detail.

"Turner, he sounds delicious."

"Is that your expert advice?"

She sighed. "Do you want me to say that it sucks being

you? I can't exactly say that. It's like you have a ton of hot guys sniffing around."

"One guy, Turner," I corrected.

"I don't care what the tabloids say about Mr. Jeremy Kalen Brinner King. Did you see that picture? The expression on his face was frosty."

"I seriously doubted he liked all the flashes of cameras going off in his face. He's a private guy."

"Keep telling yourself that."

I would, if for nothing more than to keep my sanity. I'd let him go. I wouldn't allow myself to believe I'd made a mistake. It was long past time to move on.

"What about you and Hans?" I redirected.

"Hans? Did I ever tell you the size of his penis?"

I shook my head. I missed her so much. "Um, no."

"Let's just say he gives awesome oral. Must be a skill he learned to make up for his shortcomings." She laughed. "Get it, short*cumming*s."

I couldn't help but laugh when she laughed. But then, I remembered that this was a long-distance call and not my cell phone. The community would be billed per minute for this call. "Lizzy, I have to go. But I miss you terribly."

"Tell me where you are, and I'll come."

Lizzy roughing it wasn't something I'd want to see. I loved her, but she loved things like a flushable toilet, down comforters, and other conveniences not found here.

"I'm thinking about heading home in the next few days. If not, I'll call you and let you know my plans," I said.

TWENTY-THREE

HUMMING A TUNE LOST TO MOST OF THE WORLD, something I heard often growing up, Violet continued to play with my hair.

"How much longer?" I complained.

"Hold your horses," she chided. "You can't go with your hair pulled back in a bun."

"Why not?" I could feel my brows crease in a frown.

"He's seen you every day like that. I'm giving you an elegant French twist."

Violet was worse than Lizzy. If Violet had Lizzy's stuff, I'd be used like a doll.

"Done," she said before coming around to look at me.

My frown deepened. Reaching up with both hands, I pulled at the wisps of hair hanging loose on either side of my face. "Why not just let all my hair hang free?"

She gave me a motherly look that said I should know better. "Yeah, and the old biddies will have a harvest day telling Mother about her wayward daughter."

Sometimes home reminded me of the Dark Ages. We weren't allowed to wear our hair loose in public. It was silly.

Lost in my thoughts, I missed an opportunity to stop Violet's hands before she pinched my cheeks. "Press your lips together," she dictated.

"Why?"

"Just do it," she replied. "And hurry about it."

Not wanting her to pinch my cheeks again, I did. When I looked into her eyes, her cheeks glowed with a brilliant smile. "Ready then?"

"What was that all about?" I complained.

"Nature's makeup." We weren't allowed to wear makeup. This apparently was the next best thing.

A knock came at the door, interrupting anything I might have said.

"How did you know he was here?" Was she a seer like some of the old women talked about when we were kids? I always brushed it off as stories told to keep the kids in line.

"I saw him through the window when I walked around you." She shook her head as if she knew what I'd been thinking.

The window had been to the side of me. She'd been using it for natural light to get me ready. I stood and smoothed down the skirt of my dress. My sister headed to open the door.

Turner stood and his mouth opened. He looked shocked to see me, but why? I looked the same. "You look beautiful."

I smiled brightly and began to head out the door with him when my sister whispered, "You've got that *I just had sex look*. You're glowing and rosy cheeked."

A scowl crossed my expression, which I happily gave to

her. How would looking as if I already had sex benefit me in any way this moment?

By the time we arrived in front of the town's all-purpose building, most of the families had arrived and were inside. Our hometown makeshift band played and the sound carried out into the night.

If the outsiders who were so curious about us saw this night, they'd never confuse us with the Amish again. Our leaders recognized that our youth would find other ways to busy themselves if they weren't given something to look forward to. A dance where distance between partners was scrutinized by chaperones was enough concession for even the most religious among us to be okay with.

Inside, I recognized many members, although time had changed a few faces along with the happy life that included extra padding around the middle for some. My brothers stood with my parents and the girls. I waved and Jake looked relieved.

My father said something and turned to walk away after an acknowledging wave back. My mother gave me a delighted smile and noticed that Turner held my hand. She winked and walked toward home with Piper's hand held in hers and Iris a few paces behind.

The band, which had been playing for the family affair that preceded the dance, decided a mood change of music was in order. A slow number hummed out, and Turner twirled me to land solidly against his chest. "You know, I remember our first kiss."

My cheeks flamed in remembrance. I'd barely been a teenager. "I remember," I said fondly.

He captured my gaze. "Do you? You were six." Puzzled,

I paused for a second before he got me moving again. "My parents came over to your house. Everyone cool was heading to the creek, but you clung on to me and my parents told me to stay or take you with me. I wasn't yet enamored with you. You were a nuisance."

"You weren't used to a younger sister," I teased with a wide grin.

"No, I wasn't." We spun for a second until I was lost completely in the memory. "My older brother, God rest his soul, had to put up with me." He too was caught up in things long since passed. "You wanted to play house. Which is funny now if you think about it. I guess you have a domestic streak in you."

My eyes rolled. He chucked before continuing, "I thought, well, I'll show her."

"And you kissed me," I said, it all coming back to me.

"Yes... I did." His eyes got all dreamy. "Something happened in that second our lips connected."

It had been extremely short, barely a peck on the lips. I remembered the shock I got. I thought it was static.

"You were nicer to me after that."

"I was," he answered. "I may not have known then what happened. I was only eight. But I think somehow I knew then you were my destiny. Fate put us together for a reason."

He closed his lips and focused on mine. The connection between us built, becoming palpable. He leaned in.

A tap on my shoulder made my head turn to see who was interrupting. Turner's lips met my cheek as I saw Margaret standing there. "Can I cut in?"

The vixen in me wanted to say *back off, bitch*. But this was the community, not a New York club. Using a five-letter word like that would come with harsh repercussions.

"Sure," I said, taking a step back when Turner reluctantly let go of me.

I walked to the corner and found a place to stand where I wouldn't see Turner and Margaret. No doubt she'd put on a show to try to piss me off.

Another tap came, this time to my left, and I nearly yelled, "What?" It wasn't as loud as a yell, but it was certainly rude.

Violet's blue eyes looked stunned.

"Sorry," I mumbled, unable to not be upset with Margaret's bothersome presence. "I didn't think you were coming."

"Steven didn't come home." She shrugged as if his not showing up was okay or common. No individual house had a phone, and cell phones were banned. According to my father, people lived thousands of years just fine without new technology. Thus, Steven had no way of letting her know he'd be late. I hated to give him the benefit of the doubt, but there it was.

"Where's Turner?"

I angled my head in his general direction, wishing I had a drink for the first time I'd come back home. We'd drunk the other night, but that wasn't my idea.

"Oh," she said. "I'll go get us some tea." She walked off, and I made the mistake of catching the smile on Turner's face as he laughed with Margaret.

A mild case of jealousy washed over me for a second

before I shrugged it off. I walked farther around the perimeter, looking for my brothers for whom I should have been watching. The music changed, and I told myself it was okay if Turner was still dancing with her.

Jake was easy to spot. He was chatting up the blonde girl I'd seen him smiling at days before. She too had that smile that sparkled of first love. It reminded me of what that felt like. While it was true that Turner and I had kissed when I was six, the first kiss that actually mattered was the one at the cove.

I spotted John on the fringes and began to make my way through the dancers to reach him, when a tiny girl who was little more than half his height came over to him. My brothers were tall for their age. Jake carried it like he was born that tall. But John was shyer. His broad smile brought one of my own to my lips.

"Can I have this dance?"

The request came from a very unlikely source. I turned to find Steven behind me. I had no reason to say no and graciously accepted.

"I know you don't like me," he began. "But I promise I'm in love with your sister."

"Who says I don't like you?" I asked, trying to be polite.

He hadn't done anything wrong that I'd witnessed.

"My wife and I don't keep secrets."

Now that was a lie, unless Violet had lied to me.

"Why are you here?" I asked blatantly.

He shrugged. "A better life and I found it."

"If you hurt her—"

He grinned. "I like that. Violet needs more people in her life that care about her."

I dropped my eyes, feeling like crap. Vi had been the first and not a boy. Though Father would never say it, she'd been my mother's love and his disappointment, which only got worse when I came then Mary.

Mary had weathered the storm by being everything Dad wanted in a daughter. I'd gotten attention by being my father's worst nightmare. Violet had been like a ghost, seen and unseen.

"She's loved and I'll hunt you down if you ever hurt her."

He laughed and said, "She means everything to me," before twirling me around. When I spun back to him, I changed the conversation, feeling somewhat better about the man my sister had married.

"Violet was looking for you," I said by way of conversation.

"I saw her. She's heading home."

That confused me. I was about to ask why he hadn't gone home with her when my eyes locked with Margaret who was watching me intently.

Turner was no longer with her. Since she was friends with Mary, I could only assume she'd make gossip about me dancing with my sister's husband out of spite.

"That's one thing I like about being here," Steven said as if he'd been speaking and I'd missed the early part of what he might have said.

I had no other response other than, "And what's that?"

"Women are women here. And men are men. That's something missing in America these days."

I shouldn't have been at all surprised by his answer. He probably got off on how my sister followed his every whim.

It may have been the reason he liked living here, but it was at the top of my list why I couldn't stay here forever. I did what I was told to further the community. But I would never do whatever a man asked me to do unless I wanted to.

"Lass."

We both froze for different reasons. I looked to the side of Steven and saw Turner in the distance talking to my father, which was strange. My father had left. Why was he back?

Slowly, I turned the other way and met the eyes of the devil. I faced the man I'd left behind—Kalen.

When I heard a chuckle come from my dance partner, I snapped my focus back on my brother-in-law.

"Too bad I'm going to miss the fireworks. I should find my wife."

He let me go as I thought about what he said. Earlier, he'd mentioned Vi was going home. Now he acted as if he didn't know where she was.

"Come," said the dark angel.

Kalen was beauty and wickedness all wrapped in one and my body wanted nothing more than to be consumed by him.

I folded my arms across my chest and planted my feet instead.

"What are you doing here? Are you stalking me?" I snapped.

This was starting to sound like a bad movie script.

He stood in a Henley tee and jeans. My thoughts, however, drifted to what lay beneath it all. He hadn't even touched me, standing about three feet away, yet it felt as though we were alone and naked. My center clenched and the inappropriate time was meaningless.

His lips moved and I didn't hear a word. I remembered how they'd felt against my hot skin, my heated nub, my tightened nipples and I nearly panted.

Unable to face the consequences of his being here, I stalked past him, infuriated by his non-answer.

When I passed the perimeter, I caught sight of Jake walking outside to head behind the building with the girl. Great, Father would witness my failure at such a simple duty. I was in charge of making sure my brother didn't do just what he was doing. I picked my skirt up a few inches off the ground to jog after them out the door. If they headed into the woods, I might not be able to find them in the dark.

My footfalls were silent. Just around the corner, my brother had the girl, who was probably blushing based on her posture, pinned against the wall. It brought back so many memories. I couldn't help feeling like a hypocrite, but Father was here. Both our hides would be skinned figuratively if he caught Jake.

Something stopped me—the look of absolute happiness on the girl's face. She wanted this. Hadn't I back then? The fact that we could be caught hadn't scared me. It only made things more exciting.

I turned back, taking a few steps to the mouth of the opening to hide my presence. I looked to see if anyone had followed.

He was coming for me, but no one else. I turned and saw that Jake had made contact. My focus was split between the man chasing me and my charge. When I heard the girl giggle, I faced them again. Clearing my throat, Jake and the girl looked to where I was standing. I gave them the sternest look I could muster in the midst of wanting to smile. It was the best impression of parental disapproval I could do at the moment given that I'd been just like them at their age.

Jake looked resigned and took her hand. He marched back in my direction toward the dance. His face had shut down. He knew he'd been caught. However, he probably assumed he could get away with this with me here. He'd probably asked me just for that reason.

I sighed when he reached me and gave him a half-smile in apology.

"Father's here, so be careful," I warned.

He stiffened and the poor girl looked on the verge of tears, fully understanding the consequences of their actions. Suddenly on alert, they peered around the corner first before making a dash back inside to the dance. They passed *him* on the way.

Not wanting to be far from my post, I headed back toward the side door I'd exited.

He hadn't moved, standing like a sentry posted at the door.

"You're a sight," he said, taking a different approach from earlier.

His accent was thick. It felt like years since I'd seen him last. Yet, it had been minutes and before that only a week maybe, if that. My brain was clouded with the details. I was busy trying not to combust.

"I could say the same." It wasn't what I should have said, but I wasn't thinking clearly.

Clouds of frost puffed out as we both breathed.

"Am I now?"

We were now a little over two feet apart. The urge to touch him was becoming overwhelming. "Kalen, why are you here?"

I should have urged him inside. We both stood without coats, and I should be freezing if not for his heated stare keeping me warm.

The door opened and Turner stepped out.

"Bailey, there you are. I've been looking for you. I see you met our visitor." Turner came to my side and possessively put his arm around my waist. With his free hand, he held it out. "You must be Jeremy. I'm Turner. I'll be showing you around."

Jeremy? It hit me. I'd forgotten the man wasn't Kalen. Jeremy was his first name. This night couldn't get any worse unless Turner figured out Jeremy was Kalen without me explaining things first. That would be disastrous.

Tuner gave Kalen a congenial smile. I noticed Kalen's hands clenched at his sides. I stepped away from Turner on reflex. Kalen's eyes crinkled with amusement at my action. I turned to Turner who looked confused.

"I'm sorry to cut our night short," he said slowly. I would bet he was trying to figure out what was up with me. "Your father wants me to give Jeremy a change of clothes and a quick tour. I'll come to Vi's later."

All of his words were tentative and snapped me out of my Kalen fog.

I gave him a smile that was genuine and Turner took it as a good sign. He stepped to me and placed a chaste kiss on my lips. He turned back to Kalen and didn't catch my eyes flicking to him. The man's expression had darkened like a winter storm.

Together, they walked inside to get their coats. From there I watched them leave together, all the while wondering how this was my life. Kalen shouldn't be here. My past and my present together couldn't be good.

TWENTY-FOUR

KALEN

My craving for the lass hadn't abated. With an instant addiction, I still wanted her like no drug ever known to man before. Worse, I didn't want to be cured.

I drank in the sight of her covered neck to foot. The dress wasn't the deterrent it was meant to be. Instead, it made my eyes linger longer, wanting to peel it off slowly to enjoy every inch as it was uncovered. A few fire strands of her lovely hair had escaped whatever held it back and away from her face. I pictured releasing it and watching it tumble down her back.

"You're a sight," I said. The words were gruff coming from my dry throat.

"I could say the same." Her voice was like a fist around my cock. My balls drew tight in anticipation. The idea of fucking her against the wall almost had me taking a step forward.

"Am I now?" There was nothing American left in me as I spoke. My need for her was barely contained.

"Kalen, why are you here?"

Her saucy mouth only brought out my primordial desire. That dress and our surroundings made me want to take her without further delay.

"Bailey, there you are. I've been looking for you. I see you met our visitor."

With a pleasant smile, her bodyguard had shown up and placed a possessive grip about her waist. The sight of someone touching her nearly pushed me over the edge. It was as if some psycho horror movie killer seized control of my body. I tried not to detonate. But instinctively, my hands were ready to pummel. Yet, I was able to contain them at my sides.

When the lass anticipated my next move and stepped away from the poor lad, I had to smile. She'd defused the situation, and I couldn't stop my widening grin.

She still wanted me despite her words. Otherwise, she would have stood her ground.

My competition spoke, introducing himself as Turner, and informed me he would be showing me around. If I wanted to be allowed to stay long enough to talk to her, I would have to play nice.

It took everything for me to walk away from her. I'd found her, only to be separated from her again. *Patience*, I told myself. There would be time enough to talk to her soon.

"What brings you to our community?" Turner asked.

Though he wore a congenial smile, there was cautiousness in his eyes as if he recognized the predator in me. It was a good thing. Because if he thought he had a chance in hell at keeping the lass, he was sadly mistaken. I'd never in my life claimed a woman, and now that I had, I wouldn't let her go.

"Security," I said by way of answer to his question.

That had been my excuse to be allowed in. Although they lived life not relying on technology, it didn't make them safe from the world.

His eyebrows rose, but he didn't question me further. He gave me a guided tour of what little there was to see, which wasn't much. We ended up at what could only be described as a cottage that appeared to have been built over a hundred years ago.

He showed me inside the modest dwelling and gave me clothes he thought might fit. We were about the same height and build, but I could take him if I had to. I'd never lost a fight in all my years.

He was about to show me an honest to God outhouse when a blonde came running up calling for Turner's attention.

"Give me a minute," he said, leaving me on his porch.

I took the time to take in my surroundings. It was peaceful here and reminded me a lot of home. Not having the hustle of the city, I relished the quiet as I glanced from the landscape to overhead where the clear skies were dotted with stars.

"Hi." The soft feminine voice was unexpected.

I dropped my gaze to the blonde I'd thought had left with Turner.

"I'm Margaret," she said.

Her face was illuminated only by the moon above, and it was enough to notice she was pretty. But not enough to distract me from my goal. No woman had that power, save the lass.

"I'm Jeremy."

She stepped up onto the porch and reluctantly I put out my hand to shake hers. I wasn't sure if I should be touching her. The last thing I needed was to be asked to leave before I had time to convince Bailey the merits of leaving with me without delay.

"Nice to meet you. Have you had the tour yet?"

Turner hadn't shown me much except what was along the way to where I was. With only moonlight to guide us, I wasn't sure how much more there was to see.

"Turner's planning to. He should be back soon," I said, hoping she'd leave.

"You might be waiting for a while. He's probably with her."

"Her?" Though I was sure who she was speaking of, I hoped she'd say any other name.

"Bailey, his girlfriend. He's always with her. She practically has reins on him."

I shoved my hands into my pockets to hide my fists. Girlfriend? Had the lass moved on that fast? I had to word this correctly. "I think I saw him with her earlier? They mentioned she'd only recently come back into town," which was a lie.

"Yeah, she just came back and he practically fell on his knees begging for her attention." Is that what I was prepared to do? "I'm not sure what's so special about her. She thinks she's the queen when she's not even that pretty."

Clearly, she was jealous of the lass. I wasn't sure how much of what she'd said I could believe.

When I said nothing, she finally added, "I think you'll like it around here. We're a friendly bunch. If you ever need anything, I live not too far from here. As I'm unmarried, I still live with my parents. But I can come and go as I please. They trust me to do the right thing."

Her gaze left no confusion as to her interest.

"Thanks," I said.

"I can show you around if you don't want to hang around to see if he'll come back. I have the time."

I'd dealt with enough women like her to know what she was about.

"I promised I'd wait for him."

"All right, it was nice to meet you, Jeremy. Maybe I'll see you tomorrow after chores."

I nodded and watched her walk away and tried to decide how long I would wait, if at all. I took my hands out of my pockets and gripped the railing in front of me.

The night was absolute, but so was my resolve. Bailey was mine. There was no way I would give her up without a fight.

I had a lot of questions for this Turner when he returned. The first rule of war was to know your enemy.

TWENTY-FIVE

Turner hadn't said it, but I was certain that Kalen would also be bunking at Turner's house. My father had left without incident. So there was that.

Yet, questions still tumbled around in my head. Did Father know who Kalen was to me? Or was that why Kalen told him his name was Jeremy? Or was that the name he gave everyone but me? I stood zombie-like on the fringe of the dance. Jake or John could have left and I wouldn't have noticed.

It wasn't until the band stopped playing that I came back to myself. To keep out of my head, I went to work helping to put things back along with everyone else. Once that was done, I finished my chaperone duties and walked my brothers home even though they were old enough to go themselves.

That was what Father would expect of me as guardian of my brothers for the night. I didn't go inside and instead stood several yards away as they entered the house. When they opened the door, I saw my father sitting at the table and I turned and walked away, not ready to talk to him about the community's latest visitor.

The hour was late, and besides Vi, my other option for lodging was Mary. There was no way I wanted to deal with her admonishment if I woke her baby. I trucked on to Violet's. With every step, I hoped they'd retired to their room by the time I got there.

Darkness filled the windows, not a flame in the hearth to cut through it. I stepped inside, cutting the silence with my soft footfalls. I had no idea if they were home, but it felt like they weren't.

For a second, I thought about starting a fire to banish the chill. It would only get colder as the night wore on. I opted not to and headed up the ladder to the loft for reasons I couldn't explain instead of the tiny bedroom I'd used.

I found a blanket and a pillow and made a pallet toward the back. Because the loft was open to below, I would be able to hear when my sister came home. I closed my eyes and thought over the night's events.

I'd promised Turner a chance, yet Kalen showed up. Why was he here, and what was I going to do?

I should have told the jerk to take a hike and go back to the woman he'd held in his arms. But the arrogant ass would have gotten a kick out of thinking me jealous and I was so not.

Liar. I blew out a breath of stagnant air. I was jealous and I hated myself for it. What had I learned if nothing more than men like Kalen weren't meant to be caged? Scott included himself in that category. If any man was right for me, it was Turner. I held on to that thought as I drifted off to sleep.

A hand squeezed my breast as a mouth sucked in a nipple, forcing me to wriggle. I wrapped my legs around his waist, unable to decide if I wanted his mouth or his dick to fill me. Both were equally orgasmic.

"I missed you," I whispered between pants.

He didn't speak, only worked to unlock my legs. He flipped me over and pulled my ass up high to meet his throbbing cock. Just when I thought he'd enter me, his mouth covered my mound. Long, languid strokes of his tongue across my slit teased my clit. I bit my tongue for fear of waking the entire community with an explosive release that was nearing far too soon. I couldn't complain, because history had proven it would only be the first orgasm of the night. Then he moved. His hard length replaced his tongue as he teased me with pressure against my nub.

"Kalen, I need you," I yelled in whisper tones as I fisted the blanket beneath me.

My knees escaped the pallet and rubbed against the planks of the wood floor. Something struck my leg and caused a sharp sting, smashing the fantasy.

I woke with an arm around me and jerked back in response, afraid what I might find. Tousled brown hair lifted as a face turned in my direction.

"Morning," Turner greeted, smiling at me with that damn beautiful chiseled face of his as he moved in for a kiss.

I rolled away, feeling completely wrong. I'd just been dreaming about Kalen *again*.

"Are you okay?" he asked.

"Yeah," I said, covering my mouth from the lie that just escaped it. But it did give me the perfect excuse. "Morning breath."

He grinned. "That hasn't stopped me before." He pulled me close, and I had no other excuse except the truth. His lips pressed to mine. Thankfully, he pulled back quickly. Otherwise, he may have noted my lack of response.

This only exasperated my weary mind. I couldn't do this to him. I'd become a liability to him on the verge of breaking his heart again.

In my mind, I knew Kalen couldn't offer me the stability that my heart knew Turner could. Look how easily Kalen had let me walk away, and now he was back for God knew what reason to interfere in my life.

With amusement dancing on his face, Turner said something that stopped me from moving toward the ladder. "I think you have an admirer."

I jackknifed into a sitting position and nearly bumped my head on the low wood planks that created the peaked ceiling. "Who?" I asked, praying he wouldn't say the name—

"Jeremy. Not that I blame him. He asked a lot of questions about what we were to each other."

"What did you say?" I asked too quickly. My words may have been a bit sharp. I was giving myself away.

"You two awake up there?" my sister called from downstairs. It was a dumb question because most likely she'd heard us, which was the reason for her question.

"Yes," I called out, not wanting to talk anymore about Kalen. I needed to be honest with Turner sooner rather than later. But I also needed the right words. And at the moment, I wasn't sure what to say. Turner would ask about our future and I just didn't have answers.

I scrambled to the ladder, hoping to avoid any awkwardness. Though that was what breakfast turned out to be.

Steven kept throwing looks my way like he'd pieced together who Kalen—Jeremy was to me.

Turner hadn't stayed because he had to make sure Jeremy—Kalen had something to eat.

A disturbing thought hit me. Had Kalen noticed Turner hadn't slept there? Would he have drawn any conclusions to where he might be?

I stood from my seat. "I should head out and start morning chores." Really, I didn't want to be here with Steven's probing stare and Vi's questioning glances. I made it as far as the window before Steven beat me to it.

"I'm late as well," he said, bending to kiss my sister. "I'll see you later." Then he turned and conspiratorially winked at me before leaving.

When the door closed, Vi spoke. "Steven told me about the guy at the dance. Who is he?" she asked.

There was no point in lying. "Kalen."

Her eyes became pools of frothy water. The white in her eyes enlarged around the clear blue. "He came for you."

Her words were like currents on the wind. She breathed them out like it was the end of the world. Or based on the look on her face, the beginning of one.

"I'm not sure why he's here. Turner got to him before I could ask." I pulled my hair free from its holder and twirled pieces around my finger while I gazed out the window.

"You know why he's here. The question is, what are you going to say to Turner?"

My back shifted and pressed against the cool window. "You say that like I'm going to choose Kalen."

"Well, aren't you? I saw Turner try repeatedly to get close to you this morning and you sidestepped him every time."

I swallowed. She would be too observant. "Do you think he noticed?"

She gave me a deadpan look. I closed my eyes and turned to press my forehead to the glass.

"Turner was never anything to you but a diversion. Kalen comes and Turner is chopped liver. It's not right, Bailey."

The conversation had somehow shifted and become an interrogation. I could easily say a number of things to throw in her face about her mysterious husband, but I didn't. I was guilty of several things myself. Although none of them pertained to the inhabitants of this house.

"I have to go," I said and walked out the door. I hadn't helped clean up the dishes from breakfast and felt guilty for that.

Liabilities. They were adding up. I'd been a liability in New York, and I turned out to be one here.

Lost in my own pity, I nearly walked past Kalen and Turner. Turner was talking to a group of men probably about the tasks for the day. Kalen was off to the side paying attention but not. Like a squirrel dodging a car in the street, I scampered off into the tree line, hoping I hadn't been seen. It was the gutless way. I wasn't ready to talk to either of them. Certainly not both of them together.

The snap, crackle, and pop under my feet sent me farther into the woods. I feared that my noisy steps would have Kalen or Turner turning my direction and noticing me.

It was crazy. I really needed to get over myself and face them.

The cadence of his voice stopped me mid-step. "Bailey."

I looked up into those forest green eyes of his and down to the expensive coat he wore. It didn't belong any more than mine did.

But it was the tunic beneath, revealed by his parted coat, that caught my attention. Most likely one of Turner's, it resembled the Henley he'd worn last night except instead of a button, two strings hung loose as it should have been tied at the neck as would be proper. The cream fabric was parted, giving a glimpse of his hard muscled chest. I didn't stop there. Brown trousers laced up the front hid that delicious cock of his. My mouth went dry, but I spoke anyway.

"Kalen...or should I call you Jeremy?"

We were miles apart, though we stood mere feet from each other. My body had no loyalty to Turner and was priming itself for the man before me. It was always like that with us. No other man created that kind of response. I finally understood what chemistry meant. And we had the sexual kind. The question left was if that was all we had?

"Kalen. My friends and the people who know me best call me that," he said in that lyrical accent of his.

"Jeremy then, because I'm most certainly not your friend and I don't know you at all."

"Lass—" It wasn't so much of a plea as an almost command.

I wouldn't give him time to sway me with sweet words. "Why are you here?"

His fingers combed through his hair as he let out a sigh. "Look, I'd planned to give you space. I owed you that and more. I fought the urge to find you after several unanswered calls to your cell and a trip to your apartment."

He was going nowhere, so I cut to the chase. "And that heiress?"

Muscles in his jaw flexed and I thought he swallowed. In no way did he look comfortable with this situation or our conversation. "As I recall, you said we were done. I should be asking you about him?"

The *him* didn't need a name. We both knew he meant Turner.

I looked away. "He's a friend."

He barked out a humorless laugh. "We both know he's more than a friend."

"Fiancé," I blurted without the necessary background that was needed.

His head tilted at the same time his eyes narrowed. "You said you didn't have a fiancé."

"I don't. I mean, I didn't. He was before I went to college. I left him."

"And now you're back."

The coolness in his tone rivaled the air around us. I shivered.

"It's not what you think. I didn't come here for him."

I wanted to fidget under the pressure of his stare.

"But he's here. That was the reason behind your email responses, wasn't it?"

"No... Yes... I don't know." I ruminated.

"What do you know, lass?"

I shifted my stance and found my spine.

"I know you aren't supposed to be here. And you haven't yet answered the question of why you're here."

He frustratedly rubbed at his day old stubble that just added to his devilish sexiness. He turned to the side, as if he wanted to pace. We weren't in a clearing, which made it difficult to move a foot without encountering an obstacle.

"I got information."

Exasperatedly, I asked, "And what does that have to do with me? Don't you have an empire to run?"

His body shifted and his focus again fell on me with an intensity only he could manage when he gave someone his full attention.

"This thing you found with the wires—" he began. "It was just the beginning. Someone is out to destroy me."

I let out a laugh. "And I'm supposed to believe that?"

"Yes, you are."

I waved a hand in the air. "Say that I do, so we can get this over with. Your company is wholly owned by you and not publicly traded. The Security Exchange Commission can only do so much. You're free to spend company funds as you please. The worst you could get is a slap on the wrist and lose potential investors. What does that have to do with me?"

His next words chilled me.

"Everything."

I shook my head, not wanting to believe him. "I'm just a low-level auditor—"

"Who found what wasn't meant to be found, not yet at least. You put a spotlight on a plan that was months in the making. *You* may have inadvertently saved me, as the culprits haven't pointed all fingers at me *yet*."

"So?" I said, not accepting the creeping sensation that raised the hairs on my arms.

"If those notes you received were from this same individual, you're in danger."

Now I really laughed. "How would they ever find me here?"

"I did," he said with no hint of humor.

I shook my head and did my own pacing, a step, a turn, a step, a turn before facing him again.

"My part in this is done. I'm not a threat."

"You could be. Come back to New York and I'll keep you safe."

"No way. I'm not going anywhere with you. Besides, my job is already on the line." Though I'd probably already lost it. They were just biding time to look like they were being impartial about my part in the mess.

"I'll hire you," he said, looking absolutely serious.

"For what? Sex? Because if that comes out of your mouth, God help me—"

"To clear my name."

Stunned, my mouth gaped. "What? How?"

"Follow the money just like you did in the audit. I don't trust anyone but you to find the truth."

Something in the way he spoke, I just knew. "You didn't do it."

"I didn't. Now I have to prove it," he said fervently. "My father has hired two different accounting firms, one to redo the audit, and one for overseeing future cash transactions."

"My firm isn't handling the audit anymore?" I asked absently.

He shook his head. "It was better to bring in someone totally new for both engagements."

I understood the need for independence. An auditing

firm needed to show they had nothing to gain in order to certify that financial statements were in order according to government standards. I also knew that a firm handling an audit couldn't also be consultants like temporaries in a company to oversee accounting tasks. It would be conflicting objectives.

"Who would believe anything I would find? I would only be further discredited."

"No one else would know you were working for me."

I didn't bother asking about compensation. "I can't. Honestly, that's best for you. You need someone who can stand up for you. I'm done as it is. I'll be lucky to get a job as a bookkeeper if I'm ultimately fired."

Which it looked more and more like an inevitability. I'd lost my company a client. They couldn't keep me on.

"You can't stay here."

I couldn't and not because he said it. This way of life wasn't me anymore, not that it really ever had been.

"I have Lizzy's place to go back to if I decide to."

His next statement was another crushing blow.

"Your apartment has been broken into."

Feeling like I'd been punched, I swayed. As much as I wanted to keep distance between us because my brain was cloudy enough with him five feet away, I couldn't, because that was Lizzy's place. Stepping closer to him, I nearly touched his chest when I reached out and said in a panicked voice, "Lizzy."

He took my hand, and it was like my fingers had been plunged into an electric socket. Every nerve ending in my body lit up as a shiver of goosebumps trailed up my arm and through me.

He entwined our fingers and said, "She's fine. She's still in Chicago."

"That's good," I said distractedly.

I'd talked to her yesterday, but I hadn't been sure when this break-in happened and if she'd gone home after our chat. We hadn't discussed her travel plans.

"It's fine. I have a security firm getting everything fixed up."

My first thought had been Lizzy. I hadn't considered the damage. "What did they do?"

"The first problem is that they got in. Your building has a doorman. The only other entrance is a well-lit back door that has a hidden security camera. There are more cameras throughout the building on each floor. This guy... or girl had to know about them. On top of the fact that there is a small segment of missing footage, we never see this person enter or exit the building. They couldn't be working alone."

I took a step back, not wanting to believe that I was still a target. "Wait? How do you know all of this? How did you find out about the break-in or where to find me?"

As if he could sense the weight of all he'd said was pulling me to the ground, he stepped forward and enclosed me in his arms.

He smelled woodsy like pine as I relished the strength of his arms caging me in.

"You can't go back there, not alone. Especially after they sent you black roses and spray-painted *Die Bitch* on your wall."

I jerked out of his hold as my jaw hung open.

"How did you know about the roses?" I asked. Then more to myself as my thoughts bounced around, I said,

"Lizzy." Her place had been violated because of me. "This is personal," I absently muttered.

"Yes."

A crazy thought crept in my head and though he'd yet to answer my questions, I asked another, "How did they know which room was mine?"

"Drawers were opened on your desk. They probably confirmed it by a piece of mail, according to the reports. Lizzy's room appeared untouched, as were the living and kitchen areas. Your room was destroyed, including your closet."

I felt the first of my tears. Stepping farther away from him, I mumbled more to myself, "They're just things. They don't matter."

I wiped at the stupid leakage from my eyes and was grateful I'd brought not only my laptop but my company issued one as well. Though it was likely I wouldn't have a job to go back to, I didn't want to spend what funds I had saved up to replace their equipment. Currently, both were in my car, hopefully not suffering ill effects for being locked in a frigid trunk.

"You came all the way here to tell me that," I said, shooting the messenger with all the venom I had for this psycho person or persons.

"I think you know why I came." His voice was blunt, but his eyes were soft.

"I'm in danger. Why aren't the cops here?"

"They're looking for you. I don't think you want the feds descending on your family compound. I'm sure you want this place to remain a secret."

It was true. But how did he know that? Suspiciously, I asked again, "How did you find me?"

"Griffin."

"Your driver?" I asked, confused.

He chuckled. "He's not my driver. He's a friend and owns a security firm. He has his ways of keeping up with law enforcement."

I would bet it wasn't a legal avenue.

"That doesn't answer why law enforcement isn't here for me."

"I'm sure the feds have a file on this place. They'll assume when you left, you had no intention of ever returning. However, at some point they will come around here, if you don't appear. That's another reason for you to leave."

"Leave?" It wasn't like I didn't know that I would need to. It was more of a when statement.

"The sooner, the better."

Though I'd been thinking about it, the rush to leave threw me off balance.

"I can't just leave." I shook my head and began to pace the tiny area between trees.

He stared at me like I was from Mars. "Him?"

We were trading one-word questions. It was getting ridiculous. Or maybe it was just the situation. "Not just *him*. My sister, my family. I just got here. I need a couple of days."

I expected him to rant or rage and demand I leave. His words, however, were reasonable. "You are putting everyone at risk. If I figured it out, the feds and whoever is targeting you will too."

A healthier fear would have been what he spoke about.

But I was more afraid of leaving with him and how my heart could survive the devil himself.

"Isn't there something we can do? I need a day at least," I suggested.

I hadn't seen my family in years. And there were things I needed to do before I left, including dealing with Turner.

He always seemed able to read me so easily, I thought as he spoke.

"He can come too if you'll leave this place sooner," he said with truth in his words, plainly written on his face.

Dumbstruck, I just stared at him.

"What matters to me most is that you're safe. If that means having him tag along until you both realize the inevitable, fine."

"Inevitable?"

"Yes," he said, stepping forward. "You and I are like the last two of a five-thousand-piece puzzle. We just fit together. That couldn't have been more obvious when you were in my arms just now."

I would be lying if I said my world didn't spin on its axis, leaving me feeling dizzy, but I held my ground.

"That puzzle is defective because we don't fit. The only reason you want me is for your bed or because I'm the first woman to tell you to fuck off."

I covered my mouth, suddenly conscious of where I was. Such language was not allowed, and there would be dire consequences if caught.

"You're wrong."

His utter calmness pushed my irritation button one too many times.

"No, you're wrong. I thank you for coming here to warn

me. And I'm not stupid enough to put my family in danger of exposure or otherwise. In fact, I'll leave. But I do have other friends. I can go to Chicago and stay with Matt. He's a cop and can very well keep me safe if what you say is true."

A triumphant smile formed on my lips as his formed a scowl.

"You could. But you and I both know it's not what you want. And I'm not going anywhere until you do." He kept me pinned with his gaze as his voice was barely above a whisper, yet I heard him loud and clear. "You should warn *him* about losing fingers if he continues to touch you."

I huffed out an audible sound of frustration.

"I'm not your property," I said and spun to stomp away.

Only he caught me around the waist inches away from the wide trunk of a tree. Through the thick wool of my coat, I still felt his hard cock at the base of my spine and above.

"No, you're not property. You're much more valuable than that. You're *MINE*."

He growled out the words like a final warning, and time seemed suspended between us.

"You're giving him false hope when we both know he can't give you what you want."

The truth of it got me moving. I twisted in his arms and tried to shove him away, but he didn't move a muscle. Desperate for space, I leaned back into the tree and tried to catch my breath.

"Your cheeks are as pink as your pussy after a good, hard fuck. And I intend to give you just that."

His mouth slammed onto mine with total possession. As much as I didn't want to give him entrance, I let out a gasp before his tongue invaded me like the commander he was. There was no love in the kiss. It was a little desperate and a lot angry. His hands found my hips and jerked them to him.

It took more than gravity to stop my liftoff onto my toes as his hands found my ass. The press of his cock molded against my throbbing clit and I lost all reason. When I felt air on my ankles as he fisted the fabric of my dress, I bit his lip to stop both of us.

He pulled back and wiped his mouth as his focus never left mine.

"You don't love me," I declared.

"Let me count the fucking ways."

For all his bravado, there was nothing friendly in his predatory gaze. We held there in a standoff because I couldn't allow myself to believe what I'd heard. I swallowed, trying to clear my throat so I could breathe and think at the same time, which felt impossible.

I closed my eyes because I should have been running fast and far. This man had a hold over me I didn't understand.

My eyes sprang open when the pad of his thumb traced my lips.

"You, lass, are my undoing."

"No," I asserted, shifting until his hand fell away. "You need to leave."

I ducked under one of his massive arms that had braced on the tree above my head.

"We aren't done here, lass," he said, catching my arm. "There is still more I need to say before we're not alone."

"The problem with that is, I'm done."

I cocked my head to the side, so he got my point.

He licked his lips as he took a minute as if he was measuring what he'd say next.

"You have one day to leave on your own before I take you."

He let go. My feet scraped the ground as I fled the scene, managing not one look back in his direction. He was right about one thing: my need was palpable as evidenced by the wetness between my legs. A cold shower was in order, and I headed for the sanctuary of my childhood home.

TWENTY-SIX

Dawn bloomed with a gray that blanketed the sky. A slate-colored tufted titmouse, a non-migratory bird, called a song above, and I longed for its freedom. As much as I loved my family, my home, I knew I didn't belong here.

I'd been roped into mending garments yesterday after fleeing Kalen. I hadn't had a chance to call Lizzy to check on her. I'd purposefully crashed at my parents' last night, much to my father's dismay.

Father stepped out onto the front porch just as I walked onto the worn path to the door.

"Bailey," he said. The gray of his eyes matched the pallor of the day. In them I saw that he knew just who Kalen was.

"Dad." It wasn't a term I'd often used, but it slipped out.

He hadn't asked me to come to him, so I stayed as he made his way over to me.

"That young man is really worried about you."

I nodded, knowing I should leave this place for the greater good of the community.

"I'll be out of your hair soon. I just need to take care of a few things."

His hands gripped my shoulders. "You don't have to go. We take care of our own."

It was so unexpected, tears ran like a waterfall down my face.

"I didn't think you wanted me here." The admission tumbled from my lips. My emotions grew raw over things that needed to be said. I was unable to hold them back any longer.

He sighed. "I knew since you were little you didn't belong here. But you're still my daughter. And I'll be damned if I let anyone threaten your life."

Thunderstruck, my mouth might have gaped a little and not so much at what he said, though that had been a surprise. More so by the curse word that had slipped from his tongue.

His hand came up to stroke his beard. Seeing that action too many times not to understand, I knew he was choosing his words. "Your mother was from the world out there, yet she thankfully chose to live the rest of her life in mine. When Violet was born, she was the spitting image of your mother. When you came, you had a tuff of red hair that was closer to a pale gold than the fiery locks you have now. That comes from my father's side of things. As toddlers, you both were so adventurous, I knew then I wouldn't be able to hold you back. The truth of it is, you got that from me."

I looked into my father's eyes, the man I feared, and began to see a different side of him. This was the most he'd said to me that wasn't about work that needed to be done since his speech about the birds and the bees.

His next declarative statement would be replayed in my mind over and over again. "When you decide to leave us again, you need to take Violet with you."

"Dad," I said, seeing how hard it was for him to admit this to me.

"Like you, she's meant to live a different life. I see it in her eyes. I always have."

"But she's married and seems happy," I admitted.

"She would be fine if she remained, but there is so much for her out there." He was quiet for a second. "She loves to bake. I bet she can find work or go to school for baking. We have some money saved to pay."

"Do you think she'd want to go?"

"I think she'd be afraid to go alone, but with you, she'd likely take the risk."

I didn't ask about her husband. My father was on a roll and I let him continue without interruption.

"Make peace with your sister Mary. Judge her not. She's envious that you have the spirit to leave and she doesn't. A part of her wishes she could go, but she also knows she'd never be happy anywhere else. And that's not true for you. Violet might have survived if Turner had given her his affection."

I went slack-jawed.

"You don't think we parents know what's going on? You don't think I know about the car you drove into town when you left the compound the other night, or that you're staying at Violet's and Turner's stayed with you despite the fact that I asked you to leave the boy alone?"

He exhaled as if his next words cost him. "I knew you and Turner would marry someday back when you were barely knee-high. He's a good kid and would do well by Margaret if he showed her any of the attention he shows you. I'd forgotten how smitten the boy could be until you returned. As much as it pains me to admit, he's like Violet in that he could stay or go. But he'd only stay with you. If you leave him for this Jeremy, he'll go and never look back."

That struck me. I'd always assumed he'd want to be here more than he'd want to go.

"What am I going to do?" I asked. Never in my whole life did I need his insight like I did right then.

"I can't answer that. I've never loved another woman but your mother. I will say that you and Turner remind me a lot of us. I haven't seen you with Jeremy. I do, however, see a fierceness in his eyes that rings true for all he told me."

"What did he say?"

He patted my shoulder and released me. "Some things must remain between men. I'll say that should you not choose Turner, I would give Jeremy my blessing to court you."

Shut the front door.

His head tilted to the sky. "It's going to rain and maybe snow if the temperature doesn't hold." He looked to the heavens again. "I need to get to a meeting."

"Thanks," I said, still astonished at our conversation.

"Don't thank me. Thank your mother. She wisely counseled me not to let you leave thinking that I didn't love you, lest I lose not only a daughter but a wife. Truth is, I do love you, Daughter."

And with that pronouncement, he walked off in his leisurely but steady gait.

I was still stunned. All these years, I thought my mother

was meek. Yet, my father, who was not a weak man, all but admitted that she held sway over him. If I heard him correctly, she had power in their relationship. Then again, hadn't she talked him into letting me go to college, or had she? Whatever the answers, it seemed as though she wasn't the silent partner in their marriage I'd assumed her to be, and he listened.

I went into the house and into my sisters' room to find another old dress I'd shared with Violet or Mary. Sweat and dirt clogged my pores after a day of scrubbing floors and dusting the town hall after the night of mayhem. Though there had been helpers, the place was huge. I needed to clean up for the day, as I let everything my father said ruminate in my mind.

Although my time was running out, I ate dinner at home. I still needed to talk to Turner and Violet. I wasn't looking forward to either of those conversations. Each had the potential to break my heart or hurt someone else's.

Heavy with decision, I headed to find Turner. I hadn't seen him all day, so I went to the only place I could think of to look for him, his house. Mother told me where he'd built it. And like he'd said, it wasn't far from Violet's.

On the porch, Kalen sat in a swing looking out until he spotted me.

"Is he here?" I asked by way of greeting.

He searched my eyes for things I wasn't ready to admit yet. "He left a little after dinner, probably went in search of you."

My heel caught against a rock as I went to turn. Kalen was fast and was off the porch in time to catch me just before I hit the ground. The power in his arm was magnified as he yanked me to my feet and snaked it around my waist to help steady me.

"We need to talk," he said.

"Kalen," I whispered because his touch never failed to affect me. "Please."

He stepped away, leaving me to smooth down my dress.

"Five minutes, lass." He started for Turner's front door, assuming I'd follow.

"No, not in his house."

Though I didn't plan on letting Kalen touch me, I couldn't rule out the possibility of that very thing happening. I wouldn't disrespect Turner in that way.

"Okay," he agreed.

He walked backward to the porch to grab a satchel. The tan leather was worn yet well-cared for. There had to be a story behind it the way he seemed to keep it with him. It wasn't something I'd seen him with before. However, it wasn't the time to ask.

Once he had it in his hand, he followed me around the side of Turner's house. Behind it, I stood with my arms folded over my chest. A chill crept over me now that I wasn't in his arms.

He set the bag down, careful it was within his reach. "You asked how I could love you. You need to know the ways before you walk away."

Swallowing the lump in my throat, I wasn't sure I was ready to hear this. His hand came up before it dropped back to his side. I focused on the vivid green of his eyes and the contemplative expression on his face when he spoke.

"I could say it was because you're beautiful, which is true. But I've had many beautiful women in my lifetime."

I huffed, "That's a ringing endorsement."

He wasn't rattled by my eye roll and continued undeterred.

"I could say it was because you are smart. Let's face it, that's high on my list. Nothing's worse than trying to hold a conversation with someone whose only interest is what party to attend next. But that's not it either."

Before me, he ran a hand over his thick black hair as if he were struggling with what he wanted to say. A second before he continued speaking, he stopped and looked me squarely in the eyes. "You have this fierceness in you layered by a lovely vulnerability."

I met his eyes, unsure if he would explain. I didn't have to wait long.

"You're loyal. I see that with your friend Lizzy and now with your family. You may not want to live here, but never once have you spoken a disparaging word about your family and their choices."

He paused before speaking again. "You fight for what you believe in. It would have been so easy for you to let those odd wire transactions go. But you pursued it with tenaciousness, where most in your position would have listened to their boss and not their gut and let it go."

There was nothing sweet in the way he spoke. It was straightforward and matter-of-fact.

"You believe in fair play. When you talked to me about your work, you didn't give up your client's name." I didn't interrupt to mention he was the client. "You told me enough to get my advice, but kept everything else confidential. You play by the rules."

I felt my cheeks flame, embarrassed at how he'd easily read me.

A sly grin crept on his face when he said, "See, there's that vulnerability I mentioned."

Not wanting to give in to my growing weakness for him, I spat out a snarky response,

"That's the undeniable sexual attraction between us. I feel like I need a shower and you've barely touched me. But you know that too, don't you?"

His mouth quirked, but nothing was funny. I pointed a finger at his chest and advanced. Humor lit up his face as he took steps back from my fury.

"You think this is funny, but maybe that's all we have is sex," I deadpanned, with a questioning quirk to my eyebrows. "And I refuse to be your consort, Mr. King."

The curve of his mouth flattened to a straight line. Though his back was flush against the wall, he moved like a snake strike.

"Consort," he snorted. "If you haven't already realized, you rule my heart." The damnable organ stuttered in my chest. "That's one thing Margaret had right." When had he spoken to her? A hot spike of jealousy lanced my gut. "You are a queen. You could checkmate me right now."

I'd never learned chess but knew the term and laughed. "I don't even rule your dick," I mocked, remembering that picture of him with the woman, not believing him for one minute.

Embers of fire burned in his eyes as he held on to my gaze. We could have been in Scotland by the thickness of his brogue as he spoke.

"Yer don't rule it. Yer own it." He snagged my hand and

cupped it against the hard muscle between his legs straining to break free. "I want to fuck yer and spank that pretty ass of yers. In fact, I want to yank up that peasant skirt from the dirt and ball it up around yer waist with yer legs wrapped so tightly around me there will be no beginning and ending to us as yer gaggin fer it. In fact, what I really want is yer smart mouth filled with my cock so yer dinnae say any more mince. Damn right, we have sexual compatibility. That's not all we have, though," he retorted.

He was pissed, slipping more into his native tongue. Yet somehow I got the gist of what he was saying and couldn't stop myself from egging him on.

"You really think so, because I think it's that damn commanding voice of yours that makes me want to follow *yer* every order," I mocked, in a half-convincing Scottish accent toward the end and pulled my hand free. "That's part of the reason I left this place. I *do-nae* want to be told what to do."

His lips twitched,but he held on to a glower.

Gruffly, he shook his head and said more to himself, "Tha gaol agam ort. A bheil thu a' tuigsinn na tha mi ag ràdh?"

Before I could ask him to translate, he went on and said, "There's nothing wrong with wanting to lose control, lass. For yer, maybe it's just in the bedroom where you like to be dominated."

That word. I'd heard all about that word recently. I gave him another. "I'm no sub."

"No, lass, yer not."

"And what do you know of it? Is that your thing? Because if it is, this can't work." I'd hold firm to that.

"This?" he questioned, pointing between us. "Yer admitting there's an us?"

Damn him for his accent. When it was thick like this, as if he'd stepped out of the pages of a historical novel set in the Highlands, I couldn't have wanted his arrogant bodice ripping *arse* more.

But I wasn't ready to admit defeat.

"Are you going to translate what you said?" I asked, quirking a brow.

"You said us, not me," he challenged, sidestepping my question.

"I didn't say that. I'm just letting you know that's not me."

"Aye. That's not what I'm about either," he said. "Though I admit I like orchestrating what happens in the bedroom. But I don't want to totally rule over any woman I'm with." His tone changed like we were speaking conspiratorially and he lost some of that Scottish accent I adored. "You have that fight in yer, but in the bedroom you want me to take control. I'm fine with it as are you. It works for us."

I didn't deny it. "I need tenderness too," I admitted.

"Yes, lass," he said, touching my cheek. "Right now after you've made me chase yer, I want to fuck you hard and fast. But after, I can give you slow and steady."

"Kalen," I said, removing his hand from my face.

"I know. As much as I want all those things, I won't fuck yer until I know that you're finished with him."

He straightened as if he were going to leave me there.

Unable to look at him, I stared off at the darkening sky. The sun had never made an appearance, so dusk came a lot faster.

He didn't leave. Instead, he asked me a question so slowly, the danger in it became tangible. "Have you let *him* have you?"

If I could tell a lie, I knew he might have walked away, making things so much easier.

"I haven't..." After the words were out of my mouth, I remembered what Turner and I *had* done.

"At least my thoughts of murder one have lessened to manslaughter." He chuckled at his own humor.

"I really should go find him," I said, turning to leave.

He held up a hand. "We should leave tonight."

"I haven't agreed to go anywhere with you."

His eyes darkened. "You can run, lass. But you can't hide."

I stepped off the porch, needing distance from this man before I gave in to my growing need to be closer to him.

As I walked away, he said, "I won't watch him touch you."

Before I could think of a snarky response, a yell broke in the night. "Fire." And then the bell from the schoolhouse rang.

I looked back at Kalen, and we both turned to look in the darkening sky and spotted the rising smoke. Before I took off at a dead run, I saw him bend and pick up the satchel I'd forgotten he had. What could be so important that he had to bring to the scene of a raging fire?

TWENTY-SEVEN

A BILLOW OF BLACK MIXED WITH THE GRAY CLOUDS above. A chain of people were already working as a team, sending buckets of water from the pump to toss onto the fire that threatened to get out of control.

Sick with the thought that Mary's house was lit with flames, I didn't think but took action. I snagged extra buckets from nearby houses and filled them with their pumps to help stop this before it turned catastrophic. It was possible another house would be consumed if one burning ember in the growing breeze reached a dry spot.

Then Kalen was there, taking over the job of pumping while I held the buckets to be filled. His impressive muscles worked as if he was familiar with the task.

I'd spotted Turner at the front of the raging blaze, tossing the water onto the hot spots. I didn't have to count to know everyone was here. If it was one thing our community did well, it was come together as one to overcome a crisis.

What I hadn't let myself acknowledge was that I hadn't

seen Mary or her baby. I couldn't allow myself to think they were caught inside.

By faith and by all the helping hands, the fire was extinguished before anything else could burn. Full-on darkness had almost settled in when Mary, carrying her son, came to inspect the damage to my relief. Her husband, Thomas, at her side, was covered in soot but appeared unscathed. He'd obviously been among the men who had been working hard to save their house.

Though everyone had been urged back to their homes to clean up and go on with dinner, when I caught Mary's lips trembling, it didn't matter how she annoyed me at times. She was my sister and I went to her, gathering her in a hug, being careful not to squeeze my nephew as her quiet sobs broke my heart.

When she finally pulled back, it was just family left to stare at what was left of the house.

"His room," Mary cried, pointing to the part of the house that had taken the most damage. "This is where his room is. What if he'd been in there?"

Mother went in and took my place holding Mary as I thought about her question.

My nephew was still small, and I suspected he still slept in a cradle in the room with his parents. Grief, however, was understandable, so I didn't feel the need to make that point.

"It can be fixed. It's mostly external," I said, though I was far from an expert. "Thank goodness for the rain we got last night. The wood was moist and not prime for fire."

My father agreed and he and my brothers made promises to Thomas they would be among the first to help them rebuild.

Which only begged the question as to how her house had been utterly consumed by fire.

She nodded. "Who would have done this?" she wailed to no one in particular.

That was the question. With no electricity, faulty wiring couldn't be to blame. The steady rain we'd gotten last night hadn't included a thunderstorm that could have produced a lightning strike. Furthermore, the fireplace wasn't on this side of the house. This most definitely had been deliberate.

The answer that came to me wasn't one I wanted to believe. Mary called after me. "Where are you going?" There was no time to wait, no time to explain.

My breathing was labored when I reached the house. I banged on the door until it opened.

Kalen stood with wet hair with a towel slung around his waist.

"Eyes up here," he said with amusement.

I quickly shifted my focus from the towel and the bulge there to the smirk on his face as he tapped at the corner of his eye. I pulled it together and ignored the fact that he'd caught me.

"Do you think the fire was because of me?"

It sounded stupid in my ears. How and why would this invisible person want to hurt me so badly?

He shrugged. "Like I said, it's best you leave tonight."

"And what if I brought this on? Isn't it too late for that? How can I leave them unprotected?"

"I can bring people in to watch over the place."

I pictured an army of security guys in fatigues surrounding the community.

"Kalen, you can't," I said.

"Can't what?" Turner asked, stepping into view from what must have been his bedroom. "And I thought his name was Jeremy?"

As he glanced between us, I could see his wheels turning. If he hadn't already figured it out by now, he was putting it all together.

"My full name is Jeremy Kalen Brinner King," Kalen said, not looking away from me.

"He's the guy?" Turner said.

They both waited for my answer. I nodded and Turner mimicked my action but not for the same reasons.

"He's come for you," Turner said more to himself.

"He came to warn me, and I should have listened. Mary's house is destroyed."

Turner seemed to snap out of it. "You don't know that," he said, being his levelheaded self.

Kalen ignored him and focused on me. "You need to leave and now."

Turner's head whipped around to face me. He had been watching Kalen talk. Now I saw hurt mar his beautiful face. "You were leaving without telling me?"

He didn't have to say the word *again* for me to hear it at the end of what he said.

"We don't have time for this," Kalen protested. "I will protect you even from yourself."

Turner came over and demanded an answer. "You're leaving with him?"

"What choice do I have?" A sob threatened, but I managed to hold it back.

Kalen just stood there, smug in knowing that he'd won.

"You don't even know if the fire is related to whatever's going on with you. How do you know he didn't start it to force you to leave with him?"

Turner glared at Kalen.

I swallowed, knowing it was truth time. "He couldn't have. He was with me."

Turner bobbed his head once in resignation and turned to go back through the inner door he'd come from.

"Wait," I called out, shoving past Kalen. I entered the room that turned out to be Turner's bedroom without knocking.

He stood there with his hands folded on top of his head and his back to me.

"It's not what you think."

Excruciatingly slow, he turned to face me.

"And what am I to think? That you lied to me. That your boyfriend showed up to collect you, and you're leaving with him."

"He's not my boyfriend," I pleaded.

He continued as if I hadn't spoken. "That you lied about giving us a chance."

I stepped up to him, determined to convince him of the truth. But he beat me to the punch line. "Do you love him?"

That stopped me dead. I couldn't look at him. Lying wasn't my strong suit. He didn't wait for my answer, seeming to draw his own conclusion from my silence.

"Do you love me?" he asked, voice tight.

"Yes," but it came out as a whisper.

"You can't have it both ways."

"I know."

My heart wanted one thing. My mind another.

"There's something I've been meaning to tell you," he began, causing the beating in my chest to pick up. "Before I knew you were coming, I'd planned to join a group similar to the Peace Corps. Their mission is to help communities in third-world countries survive with the resources they have."

Of course, he would. That was the man I'd fallen in love with all those years ago. He gave with all of his heart.

"Growing up here, I'm in a unique position to understand how to accomplish that having lived that way all my life. Most of the volunteers don't have that knowledge," he said.

He reached out and took my clammy hands, as I had no idea how to answer his oncoming question.

"Go with me." When I said nothing, he added, "Or I'll go with you. I'm pretty sure New York is like the jungle."

I smiled at his growing grin. "Lions, tigers, bears, and all that."

"Something like it," he said.

"I'm willing to go anywhere as long as I'm with you."

Big words from a man who had no idea who I'd become. I wasn't the girl he'd fallen in love with and neither was he the boy I'd loved. We were different, yet the same.

I knew I could trust my heart with him even if the traitorous thing had other plans. But that particular part of my anatomy had made all the wrong decisions in the past. Maybe it was time to listen to my brain. If I'd done so from the beginning, Turner would be my husband and Kalen would be a social media headline I would have missed.

"Don't answer now," he said. "Think about it. Above it all, I want you to be happy."

He placed a chaste kiss on my forehead, drawing me

close. There, I felt like home.

Unfortunately, there were only flickering sparks, not the all-consuming need to drop my clothes and give myself to him. In his defense, I didn't feel that hardness I also felt in Kalen's arms.

What did that matter? Turner and I had passion. I'd given him my virginity and spent many stolen moments finding pleasure with him. *I don't have to be consumed by another man to be happy*, I told myself.

Turner's hand slid down my back and I felt him begin to grow hard.

He stepped back, looking faintly embarrassed. And that was okay. He was a man who'd grown up to treat women with respect, not like the barbarian Kalen was. Yet, I couldn't deny a little disappointment that he hadn't lost control because of me.

Every time Kalen needed me with such voracity there was power in it. I felt in control, wanted, desired.

"I should go check on Mary," I said, wanting to end any embarrassment on either of our parts.

Turner did something unexpected. He got in my space and walked me backward until we reached the door.

"Make no mistake how much it's costing me to hold back. I want you. But *all* of you. I've waited years. I can wait another day for you to decide."

This time, I'd felt all of him and his desire for me as a long, hard fact.

His lips brushed over mine a second before he stepped back.

More confused than ever, I scrambled out the door and found Kalen dressed and waiting for me.

TWENTY-EIGHT

KALEN STOOD BY THE TABLE WITHOUT A SMILE, SMIRK, or anything in between. He was expressionless and I sighed, not ready for round two.

"You'll need this when we leave," he said, pulling a small purse from the leather satchel.

Curious, which had always been my downfall, I moved closer and took it from his hand.

"What is this for?" I asked, eyeing the salmon-colored Prada labeled bag he handed me. "Do you think because people can't name the color of this that they'll be so busy staring at the purse rather than at me?"

The glare he threw at me hadn't been what I'd been going for. "Open it," he demanded.

I unzipped the sporty purse whose color was somewhere in the pink family. I decided not to comment on the fact it was a designer bag that probably cost more than the combined wardrobe for the entire community.

He knew that it cost too much. It didn't need to be said. I pulled out eyeliner and mascara. There was more, but I got the point. "Makeup, really? I don't wear that much as it is. My guess is that it would draw more attention to me."

"Keep looking," he said, sounding annoyed.

Fumbling around in the purse until I felt something that didn't feel like makeup, I pulled out a bottle. "Hair dye." Black at that.

"It's not permanent."

"Why?"

"We thought it best you hide in plain sight," he said.

"We?"

"Stop deflecting," he said.

"And the makeup..." I trailed off, remembering the TV image of Kalen with the heiress. I'd only caught the briefest of views, but it wasn't something I could forget. Her hair had been black. "The woman in the pictures. Is that why you were with her?"

Silently, I pleaded for that to be true.

"No. I wasn't lying when I said I was giving you space," he admitted.

Then it all made sense. "I'll look like her, so when I'm going into your apartment people won't expect it to be me."

Something snapped inside me. The thought of another woman in his space making love to him killed a part of me. My fist connected with his chest before I let him have it with my words. "You bastard. A couple days after your declaration of love, you took her to your bed."

He stilled my beating fist, makeup falling from the open bag to the ground. "She cares," he said, but the *she* to whom he was referring was me.

"I don't," I answered, pulling my hands free, picked up the spilled makeup and then shoved the purse into his chest.

"I'll drive to the airport in the morning and catch a flight to Chicago."

I didn't think I could afford to pay cash for a last-minute flight. But I did have an emergency credit card I hadn't used.

"Whoever it is will follow you."

"It doesn't matter. Isn't that the point, to draw them away from my family?" I spat.

"Fine. We leave together." He shoved the purse back at me. "You and all that fuckable red hair will leave, and if someone is watching they'll take the bait. But when you get to the airport, you'll find one of those family bathrooms tucked away somewhere and change your appearance."

"No," I declared. "I'm not running scared."

"Then I'll follow you wherever you go."

"What about your son?" I said, checkmating him.

He stopped for a moment, probably taking stock of what I'd said.

"He's protected," he said finally. "But know this, lass. For no other woman would I leave him. Only for you."

Though I still didn't allow myself to believe him, I took the purse because he wasn't going to let me go without it.

"I have to go check on my sister Mary," I said.

"I'm coming."

I shook my head. "I'll go to Vi's and have Steven walk with me. She's not that far. You can watch me from the porch if you want."

He said nothing but followed me outside. The moon was hidden, so it was true dark. Still, there was a vague shape of my sister's house off in the distance.

"Goodnight," I said and glanced over at Turner's door.

I wondered how much he'd heard. Then again, it wasn't like he had a TV or radio to drown out our conversation. So all of it, I assumed.

Before I could get off the porch, Kalen said, "You could always come back and we could finish what we started before."

An invisible *yes* neon sign lit up in the vicinity of my crotch area, but I didn't stop, knowing I would likely give in to his offer.

TWENTY-NINE

SELF-PRESERVATION WAS HIGH ON MY "TO-DO" LIST. I found myself jogging most of the way to my sister's house.

When I entered, she sat alone in the kitchen.

"Where's Steven?" I asked.

She pointed toward their room. "He's asleep. Fire or not, there is work to be done in the morning."

I nodded.

A faint hint of a smile grew on one side of her face. "So he's the guy?" She waited for me to answer. "The visitor?"

I sighed. "He's the guy."

"Well damn, Bailey."

My eyes widened. I'd never heard my sister say one foul word.

She waved me off. "Don't act like you've never said it. Besides, he's handsome."

That was an understatement.

"Two good-looking guys. What are you going to do?"

"Leave and you should come with me," I said.

"You're leaving with Kalen—Jeremy? Whatever his name is."

I ignored that and got right to the point.

"I'm pretty sure the fire is my fault."

It was her turn to look shocked. "The trouble in New York."

"Yes. I don't want anything worse to happen. And Father suggested you go with me."

Her jaw stayed unhinged. "What, and leave Steven?"

"If Steven loves you and has nothing to hide, he'll go with you. You don't belong here any more than I do."

Everything Father had said made sense.

"And what would we do there?" she asked dryly.

I rolled my eyes. "I don't know about Steven, but you can bake."

"Yeah, like that's hard."

She had no idea.

"I can't bake," I said.

"You can if you put some effort into it."

I shook my head. "I'm not going to argue with you. You can make a life there. Father's offered to pay for you to go to baking school or cooking school, whatever they call it."

"No fooling?"

My head rocked side to side.

Hers did the opposite. "I'm not going anywhere."

My vision narrowed. "What?"

"Not without talking to my husband."

I couldn't blame her for that.

"I get it, but I can't stay," I pleaded. "I'm leaving in the morning."

"I'm not going without Steven," she said firmly and

stood. "Thank you for talking with Father. Though I may not love it, I do like my life here."

I smiled at her, and she turned and went into her bedroom. I'd forgotten to ask about Mary. If she wasn't staying here, she most likely was staying with one of her friends.

According to my father's wishes, I was to make peace. With little time left, I wasn't sure that was possible. It was too late to call on her.

I sat at the table and closed my eyes. Before Kalen had shown up at the dance, I had settled with my decision. Or was I settling?

Both men would be desirable to any woman. Handsome and sensual. Even though they were different, they possessed some of the same qualities.

My love for Turner had stood the test of time. He was solid. Someone I could trust who would never do anything to break my heart.

Everything with Kalen was new and exciting. It was akin to the budding of first love. It held mysteries still left to unravel.

Still, I grew certain of what I was going to do.

A thunderous boom and a flash of lightning pierced the night. A second later, the sound of an assaulting rain drowned out everything else. I sat there for a few minutes before deciding to head to bed.

Just as I got to my feet, the door opened, letting in a fierce wind and blowing rain. I was caught in the blast, my face dotted with raindrops.

A sloshing mass of a wet man stepped through the door, pitch blackness behind him. I looked toward my sister's closed door and heard no movement in the short silence.

The figure glanced in that direction before turning intense eyes on me. My sister was fine. I was the one in danger.

He stomped forward, the storm masking the noise of his footsteps. I backed up, unwilling to be in a defenseless position when he faced me not a foot away.

His beautiful face was plastered with wet hair. I was unable to stop my hand from pushing the limp strands from his face. I cupped his cheek and stared at my expression in the pools of his eyes that danced in the light of the fire. He leaned into my touch.

Silently, I felt his determination for me to choose him. It broke the wall I'd erected around my emotions and carefully hidden heart.

The rain that dripped down my face mixed with tears as I accepted what was to come next. I stepped into him slowly. When we were flush, I stood on my toes and kissed first one cheek then the other. I tasted the unmistakable saltiness of tears—mine or his I didn't know when I pressed my lips to his. I drew his face closer. It didn't matter that his wet clothes dampened mine.

My fingers moved from his face down the hard plains of his chest and down to the top of his pants. I tugged the offending article of clothing free of them. Droplets of water sprang out, and I managed with his help to get his shirt over his head.

His hands reached around my neck and began to undo the buttons at my back. When he finished, he parted the fabric, separating it to my shoulders, freeing my arms. I stood exposed in a manufactured bra from the waist up as my skirt clung obstinately to my hips.

Next, I managed to undo the front flat of his pants. With one good push, they fell with the speed of gravity to hit the floor, creating a puddle of fabric and water. At the same time, his cock sprang free, giving little doubt that his intention matched mine.

His hand reached back up to my neck and his fingertips glided down my back, to pop the clasp on my bra with expertise. Letting my arms hang at my sides, it fell to my feet. I shivered as much from the coolness of his damp fingers as the touch itself. He pushed my dress and my underwear down as one. They hit the floor with a silent splat.

As a unit we took two steps back away from the clothing that had confined us moments before. His lips touched mine as our bodies melded together and he continued to dance us back to the rug in front of the fire.

My hands went to his shoulders and pressed down, letting him know my objective. He surprised me by lifting me up. Hands urged me up to wrap my legs around his waist, trapping his rock-hard cock against my core to create delicious pressure.

My orgasm was so close it could be counted down beginning with "T minus ten" for liftoff and we hadn't really begun yet.

Too much sexual tension had been building that needed release.

Unfortunately for me, we hadn't ended up against the wall, which had become a favorite position of mine. Instead, he knelt with me still wrapped around him.

When my back met the rough tread of the rug, I barely registered it. My arms wove around his neck, drawing him in for a real kiss, the prelude to everything to come. He tongue fucked me with all the promise of what was to come. I relaxed my legs, giving him room to push inside me in the most exquisite way.

He had different ideas. He trailed a line of hot kisses down my neck to my collarbone, only to continue to a breast. He suckled it and I bit my tongue, knowing we were not alone in the house.

The idea of us getting caught only heightened every sensation as I arched my back off the floor. He paid homage to the other breast, eliciting the same response. When his hands trailed down my sides, along with more kissing and licking, I squirmed with the oncoming penetrating sensations.

Pay dirt happened when he played tic-tac-toe down the center of my body. First was the capturing of my clit with his lips and a gentle nip with his teeth. Then his tongue thrust inside me, making me rise up on my elbows to look down at him. When his tongue flicked a little lower, my head fell back, nearly cracking the floor. His fingers moved inside my core while his tongue continued to tease an area I wasn't sure I'd make available to anyone else. I couldn't think very well past the pleasure.

His thumb teased that entrance, and my body grew wetter still. His tongue moved back as if eager to lap up all I had to offer. Just when I was about to call out and beg him to fill me with his length, I held in a moan as I rode out my orgasm. His fingers worked in and out, drawing out my release.

When I could no longer hold myself up to watch this magnificent man's magic, he rose up. Muscles corded with his movement as he crawled to place the head of his shaft at my opening. Slowly, he pushed inside me.

My cry was stifled by his kiss. Thankfully, the storm outside continued to rage on and provided the cover we needed. But neither one of us seemed to care that my sister or her husband could walk in on us.

I tasted my orgasm on his tongue and that strangely wound me up again. I rocked my hips, urging him forward, but he took his time. His eyes were closed tight and our kissing stopped, as he seemed to be holding back as if memorizing this moment.

When the tip of him hit the end of me, there was a confusing moment between pleasure and pain. He pulled back, not as slow, but not fast either, before he moved back in. It was like he was being careful, but I didn't want or need that. I bucked my hips a couple of times before his eyes opened wide and he began moving in earnest. Rolling his hips, he dragged the tip of himself against that spot deep inside that made me thrash.

Although his pace had picked up, I was in need of something faster and harder. I met his thrust, trying to force his pace when he finally broke and gave me what I wanted. He thrust in me with purpose, hard and deep, hard and deep, his eyes colored in the amber light from the fire that crackled beside us. I came again, and it seemed to last a lifetime. Just when the waves that crested over me began to subside, he came in a guttural thrust.

When he went limp on top of me, it was only a moment before he rolled so we lay side by side. Still inside me, he kissed me with a sweetness that didn't match the furious lovemaking seconds before.

But there in his arms, I finally found the peace that had evaded me for days.

When I woke, he was on his back with me tucked at his side. He'd covered us with the afghan from the couch, but I still shivered. The fire had burned down to nearly embers, leaving a distinct chill in the air. I got up to get a blanket from the room I'd been using. I snagged the first piece of clothing I came across, his still damp shirt. But without much light, I didn't want to search and be caught naked.

After grabbing the blanket, I draped it over him before listening at my sister's door. The faint sounds of breathing could be heard. I wasn't sure of the time, as the sky was still dark, due to night or cloud cover, I wasn't sure.

I crept back over to the man who had loved me in ways I would never forget. I stared at him a second longer before peeling off his soggy shirt. I began to dress, putting on my bra and panties, then my dress before adding another log and kindling to the dying fire.

Then I picked up his clothes and draped them over the side of a chair nearest to the hearth to help dry them. He hadn't stirred, whereas I felt restless.

I struggled with what I'd done. I didn't regret it, only the fallout to come. I walked out the back. The rain had ended sometime in the night. It was very cold and the reality I needed. Snow was falling lightly as the midnight sky began to lighten to a storm cloud day as the sun began its appearance on the horizon.

I thought about the man inside and my tears burned hot paths down my face. My tears weren't only for him. I cried for the other man who would never forgive me when he found out what I'd done. Whereas I'd wanted so badly to stay in that bubble in time and not face the truth of the day.

The need he'd come to me with couldn't only be answered with a choice. Any choice had the potential of breaking me, but I made it anyway. I hoped we'd all be able to live with that decision. There was no forgiveness for this transgression.

My steps made lasting impressions in the new fallen snow. A gentle breeze moved what was left of the unharvested cornfield to sway as if in a dance. The sounds that played through the abandoned stalks left to feed the animals were its own melody. It sang of love and loss, no right or wrong.

When the rays of the day fully emerged from its slumbering, penetrating the heavy clouds, light created a beam across the fields. I turned to go face the song of betrayal that awaited me.

A swishing sound had me looking back.

THIRTY

KALEN

Everything was wet as I stared around the room. I'd walked in and found the house empty. Bailey was gone and the door to her room had its own mind when it broke free of my hand and banged open as I searched for her.

Turner walked in minutes later, all innocent. I asked in a volume that could wake the dead, "Where is she?"

"Huh?" he said with utter confusion.

My mind raced with possibilities I didn't want to consider. I checked my rage and said again, "Where is Bailey?'

"I don't know?" he uttered, sounding puzzled.

Had he said, *she changed her mind, she's not leaving with you,* I might have pummeled him. We both looked at the wet clothes spread out on a chair and the lass' bonnet left near a pile of blankets near the fire. Neither of us acknowledged the fact, though there weren't many possibilities for how Bailey had spent her night.

Having never been in love before, the tightness in my

chest first made me think heart attack. It may have been out of the norm for someone my age, but not impossible.

"Did she leave?" Turner asked, disappointment etched on his face.

"Or did she just run?" *From the both of us*, I thought.

I'd told the lass I'd loved her and asked her if she'd understood. Though I'd done it in Gaelic, maybe somehow she had.

"It's early, but maybe she went to help with morning chores at her parents' house."

I shook my head. "No, she knew we had to leave this morning." Then I just said it. "She must have run," I whispered the words, but he'd heard them anyway.

"No, she promised she wouldn't," he said but didn't look convinced.

"But that's what she does," I said. "She ran from you, she ran from Scott, and then she ran from me."

I watched him as he put the pieces together. "We need to check if her car is still here."

No other words were needed. There was still an undercurrent of unease. We practically ran to the other side of the community to the security station. My daily workout sessions had paid off. I was barely breathing heavy when we came to the brick building to find my sports car and another.

"That's her car." He looked over at mine. "You know she's not impressed by money," he declared before heading inside the building that was the only halfway modern-looking one in this whole compound. I followed after I patted my side to find I'd left my bag at Turner's.

In the security station, Turner asked the guard, "Have you seen Bailey?"

"No," came from a heavy accented voice. It was Southern, I think they called it here in the States. "And no, she didn't call a cab," the voice continued.

Turner looked on the verge of leaving. I wasn't sure if this question had been asked, but I said it anyway, "No cars came down this path at all today?"

I viewed the bank of monitors in front of the guy. Based on the comments I'd heard, this security was to protect the compound from the curious, not the crazy.

"Yeah, a car showed up, drove down, and turned back without stopping. But that's not unusual," the guy said defensively. "People accidentally turn on that road and ignore the private sign all the time."

"How often does that happen?" I queried.

"Once or twice a month."

Gritting my teeth, I continued, "And what time did this happen?"

"Oh, about an hour or two ago."

On the verge of hitting someone, I ignored him and focused on Turner.

Beating me to the punch, he said, "I still think she could have gone home."

"Is there a problem?" the guy asked. He looked as if we'd woken him from a nap. His blond hair was muddled every which way. "Should I contact Mr. Glicks?"

"No," Turner said. "I'm heading over there now."

We exited the building and our brisk walk turned into a jog.

After giving the story to Bailey's mother, all three of us headed back to Violet's. After we made it back, Bailey's mother, convinced no one was home, left in search of Violet and her husband to see if they'd seen her.

I'd already sent a message to Griffin to look into Steven's background. I'd learned that he was new to the community and hadn't yet been located. Though I didn't want to believe he had anything to do with Bailey's disappearance. He couldn't have known Bailey would show up here, could he?

Not wanting to scare Bailey's mother, we'd suggested the possibility that Bailey had probably gone for a walk.

When the back door banged open and closed from a breeze, both Turner and I lunged in that direction.

We both looked at it first, hoping it just hadn't latched, but that was a long shot. Outside, I caught sight of something not right. "Look over there."

Turner's eyes followed the direction of my finger. He was about to shrug it off when he really got a look at the disturbance in the stalks. "Where does this go?"

There was a set of footprints in the snow. One that led toward the field and began to come back. And there was something else.

We started walking forward, neither of us wanting to believe what may be true.

"This is our natural barrier to the public road that is about a half a mile straight ahead. And the stalks run about a mile parallel to the road. It keeps people from wandering in here in summer and feeds the animals in winter. The stalks are tall, and it's easy to get lost when in season."

The stalks were tall, taller than me, but limp. They blended in like a forest of tan. Still, it was easy to see a trail of broken stalks someone left in their wake. The width of the path suggested that someone was probably carrying something while trampling through.

We traded looks before we took off. It was easy to navigate with the path already made for us.

In a couple of minutes, we'd made it to a road. What I saw chilled me. Tire tracks were left in the muddy snow on the side of the road. It appeared someone had been parked here. And most likely they had Bailey with them.

I saw fear in Turner's eyes that mirrored my own.

"Whoever it was could be anywhere now, most likely on a highway headed out of state," he declared.

"There have to be cameras that may have spotted something."

His response to me was, "We don't even know what kind of car it was."

My answer was to look at the tire tracks, knowing he was smart enough to get it. Tires were manufactured to fit only specific vehicles. We could narrow the possibilities down considerably, given the right forensic tools.

Out of my pocket, I pulled my sat phone. I caught Turner eyeing the device before he spoke. "I guess there are things you can do for her that I can't. Are you calling a team of professionals to find her?" His voice was laced with bitterness. Fear had a way of letting one's true emotions show through.

Matching my tone with his, I said, "You aren't the only one who cares deeply for her."

He rolled his eyes and swept the street instead of looking at me. I dialed a number. With dawn only recently coming to pass, I glimmered a bit of satisfaction when a groggy voice answered. It was the small things that kept one sane in times of crisis.

"What?"

"It's Kalen." I kept it to the point.

There was a pause before the voice said, "Bailey's Kalen?" There could have been pleasure gained in that question if it was true.

"Yes," I answered in the affirmative. No need for clarification at this point.

"Why are you calling at this ungodly hour?"

Not wanting to waste time, I kept it simple. "You remember that audit issue she found?"

"What now, you want me to help locate the people who did it?" I could hear amusement in the voice that said I would need his help.

"No, I want you to help locate Bailey... Matt, she's been taken."

<<<<>>>>

PART THREE OF THE KING MAKER SERIES IS
COMING DECEMBER 2019

THANK YOU

I'd like to thank you for taking the time out of your busy life to read my novel. Above all, I hope you loved it. If you did, I would love it if you could spare just a few more minutes to leave a review on your favorite e-tailer. If you do, could you be so kind and **not leave any spoilers** about the story? Thanks so much!

ACKNOWLEDGMENTS

Writing is not a right as much as it is a privilege. I wouldn't have that opportunity to do this if not for my readers. And I've been doing this now for a decade now, and I'm grateful for all the support my readers have shown me over the years. So THANK YOU.

THANK YOU TO my beta readers. They are first look that everything I think I got on the page actually made it there:

Kelly Reed-Brunet— Thanks for always being there at a moments notice. YOU ROCK and are a true friend!!!

Thank you to my writing partner Anne Hargrove. You are always there to help no matter what in my time of need. Thanks bestie.

Thanks to Michele @ Michele Catalano Creative, always sees my vision even before I know it. Thank you for squeezing me in and designing a beautiful cover.

To Sara, thanks for your fantastic photography.

Thank you to Paige Smith. You are always there last minute to work me in. You give shine to my words.

Thank you to Rosa Sharon at iScream Proofreading Services for your keen eye, extremely fast turnaround, and always being there short notice.

ABOUT THE AUTHOR

Terri E. Laine, USA Today bestselling author, left a lucrative career as a CPA to pursue her love for writing. Outside of her roles as a wife and mother of three, she's always been a dreamer and as such became an avid reader at a young age.

Many years later, she got a crazy idea to write a novel and set out to try to publish it. With over a dozen titles published under various pen names, the rest is history. Her journey has been a blessing, and a dream realized. She looks forward to many more memories to come.

STALK ME AT

Facebook: terrielainebooks
Facebook Page: TerriELaineAuthor
Twitter: @TerriLaineBooks
Instagram @terrielaineauthor
Goodreads: terri e laine
Newsletter Signup:
https://www.subscribepage.com/terrielaine

I have several upcoming releases, make sure to sign up for my newsletter or check my website for details.

www.terrielaine.com

ALSO BY TERRI E. LAINE

Because Of Him

Captivated by Him

Chasing Butterflies

Catching Fireflies

Changing Hearts

Craving Dragonflies

Songs for Cricket

Ride or Die

Thirty-Five and Single

Sex, Alcohol, and My Neighbor (in Beer Googles Anthology)

Honey (formally Vault Anthology)

Sugar

Married in Vegas: In His Arms

Absolutely Mine

Money Man

QUEEN OF MEN

other books co-authored
by Terri E. Laine

Cruel and Beautiful

A Mess of A Man

Made in the USA
San Bernardino, CA
10 January 2020